The Devil's Canyon

Kirby McBride doesn't hesitate to accept a plea for help from the old Texas Ranger commander who once saved his life. Colonel Tremaine plans to revive his dwindling cattle ranch by driving steers north from Don Trujillo-Lopez's drought-hit Mexican holding to his own heavily grassed range before they can be sold and the profits split.

But the dangerous Luis Escobar has his eye on the cattle as well as the Don's dark-eyed daughter, Angela. As Kirby starts the great herd north with Escobar in pursuit, both groups are aware of another deadly threat.

Now there will be a deadly confrontation in the desolate Devil's Canyon. Who will be left standing?

The Devil's Canyon

Owen G. Irons

A Black Horse Western

ROBERT HALE · LONDON

Typeset by
Derek Doyle & Associates, Shaw Heath.
Printed and bound in Great Britain by
Antony Rowe Limited, Wiltshire.

ONE

The wind was cold off the north. The sky was blue between clusters of swift-moving high clouds above the North Texas plains. There was a long valley covered with bright green grass below. The wind flattened the grass and turned it silver as it blustered southward. The mane and tail of the big gray horse Kirby McBride was sitting whipped in the gusting wind as well. Kirby shifted in the saddle and sat leaning his hands against the pommel studying the land. He could see the glint of a small pond further west and around it a grove of mature live oak trees. It had been a long ride, but maybe it had been worth it.

Colonel Tremaine hadn't exaggerated in his letter. It was a fair, lush country. The problem was, as any cattleman would notice immediately, there weren't but a hundred or so cattle scattered across a valley that could easily graze thousands.

The gray gelding lifted its head and pricked its ears. Some sound Kirby hadn't heard had caught its attention. Perhaps other horses, nickering distantly.

'It won't be long now,' Kirby said, patting the gray's neck. 'We'll get the saddle off and find you some feed.'

It had been a long ride for the horse as well. Five hundred miles or more, most of it across arid country with poor graze through some bad weather. The threat of the Comanches had been constant. That and the almost equally dangerous threat of prairie dog holes where the big gray could snap a leg and leave Kirby on foot.

Kirby unfolded the well-worn letter Lou Tremaine had sent him in San Angelo, glancing at the roughly drawn map. The house should be just beyond the oaks and the gleaming pond. He kneed the horse and they started forward down the long, grassy slope.

The house, when he came upon it, wasn't much as yet. Log and wattle, sod roof. Sawn lumber was hard come by in this country. But Kirby could see where Tremaine had been laying out ground plans to expand his house.

If he ever got cattle enough to pay for the additions. That was the reason Kirby was here. Of course, he would have gone anywhere at anytime to pay back the debt he owed to his former commanding officer.

Four men stood around the pole corral, watching as Kirby rode the weary gray slowly across the yard of the ranch house. Another man stood inside the corral holding the lead to a trembling, frothed horse, apparently a mustang newly broken, for it was exhausted, head hanging. It had streaks of blood along its bay flanks where it had been cut by spur rowels and Kirby's mouth tightened just a little with disgust. There was no need to do that to a horse, even when breaking it.

'Afternoon,' he said as he drew up, looking down at the men. 'Is the colonel around?'

'He won't be back for awhile,' one of them answered. He turned his head and spat, still leaning casually against the corral rails. He was bulky, with a low forehead. His red shirt was torn at the elbows and sun-faded.

'I'm ramrod here,' he told Kirby, 'Asa Donahue.'

No hand was offered and Kirby just nodded. Slowly then he swung down from the gray's back. He felt numb from the waist down. His lower back had a kink in it.

'Where can I stable up my horse?' he asked Donahue.

'Out on the prairie if you like,' Asa Donahue answered expressionlessly. The narrow cowboy with the long black mustache beside him laughed out loud.

'You don't understand,' Kirby said mildly, already disliking the big man, 'I'm staying here. My name's Kirby McBride. Maybe the colonel mentioned I was coming.'

'Maybe he did . . .' The expression in Donahue's dark eyes changed, his eyebrows drawing together. 'McBride? Ain't I heard that name before?'

'It's a common enough name,' Kirby said. He was loosening the double cinches on his Texas-rigged saddle, hat tilted back now. He smiled at the others.

'I'll talk to you all a little later, boys. I'm the *new* ramrod.' He glanced at Asa Donahue whose face went as hard as stone, touched the brim of his hat and turned away, leading the gray toward the stable.

Asa watched him go, his cold eyes set and glittering.

'I guess that's that then, Asa,' the man with the mustache said as they watched the tall man leading his horse across the yard. Asa spun on his companion angrily.

'You think so, Len? Do you!'

'You heard what he said. . . .'

'Shut up. I'm thinking.'

The redheaded cowboy who had been in the corral slipped through the rails and stood coiling up his lasso.

'Is that who I think it is?'

'I don't know,' Asa said, in a hoarse whisper.

'He gave his name as McBride, didn't he?'

'Yeah, but he looks too young to be that one, don't he?'

7

'Maybe,' Red said shrugging. 'May be him, may be kin.'

Asa continued glowering. Abruptly he made up his mind. 'It don't matter who he is. He's leaving, and now!' He took three purposeful steps toward the stable, his hand resting on the butt of his holstered gun, the others lagging behind.

They halted suddenly because from under the large oak trees to the north the tall man on the silky roan appeared unexpectedly.

His hair and mustache were silver. He sat ramrod straight in the saddle. His strange blue-gray eyes were looking at them, studying the situation. And Colonel Lou Tremaine was not smiling.

'Better get back to work,' Len said to their leader in a low voice. 'The colonel doesn't look happy.'

Asa hesitated a moment, still staring at the open stable door and then he nodded. He lifted a hand to the approaching ranch owner, a gesture to which Tremaine did not respond, and then the three cowhands scattered to attend to various chores.

Kirby McBride stood hatless in the shadows of the stable, the open door framing him, his curly dark hair across his forehead. His hands were on his hips and there was a grin on his face as he watched Tremaine's slow approach.

The colonel looked older, of course, but no less trim, no less resolutely in command. He took the reins to the colonel's horse as Tremaine reached the stable and the older man swung down.

The colonel stood studying Kirby for a long minute, taking in the well-set-up shoulders, boyish blue eyes where a hint of menace also lurked.

'Let's go inside, Kirby. Someone else can put the horse away.'

And that was his greeting after five years to Kirby

McBride. Kirby smiled inwardly. No, the old man had not changed a bit. He never would. There was little room for emotion in Colonel Lou Tremaine's world. You went out, did a job, expecting no thanks from anybody for doing your duty.

He had fought for five long years in the War Between the States, later six more against the Indians and outlaw bands of Texas.

If the colonel ever laughed, Kirby had never seen it during their two fighting years together. He barely smiled; when he did it was a knowledgeable smile as if he and he alone understood the foibles of mankind and he reflected on these with ironic detachment.

He was a man of a fading breed. Inflexible, maybe, but fiercely loyal. The old man would lay down his life for a cause he believed in, and for a friend.

He had proven that before. If it weren't for Tremaine, Kirby would have been dead at Anchor Wells when a band of Comanches jumped their Ranger detachment.

'It's not much yet,' the colonel said, as they reached the plank porch of the house and stepped up, 'but I have hopes.'

He slipped the latchstring and they entered the strongly built, low-roofed house. The room they had entered had Indian rugs scattered on the packed-earth floor for decoration. The roughly built stone fireplace was massive. Above the mantel an old Spencer carbine hung in brackets. Two huge upright supports braced the low ceiling. The windows were small, flanked by swing-shutters with firing slots cut into them. The furniture was sparse enough: three heavy home-hewn chairs, all facing the fireplace. And beyond, a puncheon table, seven feet long with an array of stiff wooden chairs around it.

'I'll be putting wooden flooring down soon,' the colonel said, nearly to himself, stamping on the earthen floor with his polished cavalry boot.

'It'll do, sir. In time it will do just fine.'

Kirby stood, hat in hand looking the place over. The colonel sighed, removed his own hat and wiped back his gray hair.

'In time . . . come to the table and sit down, Kirby. I've got some coffee. And we've a lot of talking to do.'

They sat at the big table and Tremaine poured them each a cup of coffee. The colonel studied Kirby in silence for quite some time, then as if he had made his final decision, he said, 'You've looked the ranch over?'

'Just what I could see riding in. A handsome piece of land, Colonel.'

'Yes? And?'

'Damn few head of cattle.'

The colonel nodded. 'Unfortunately, you're right, Kirby. That's why I wrote asking you to come out here.'

'Oh?' Kirby's eyebrows lifted slightly. He let the colonel continue in his thoughtful way.

'We have had some luck. You have to understand,' Tremaine said, leaning back in his chair, 'the past three years this land was dry and sere, short yellow grass, and so little of that the steers were practically fighting each other over graze. Then the rains began, good soft rains soaking gently. I could see the country going green, and I knew I was going to have a good growth of grass.'

'But still the same number of cattle,' Kirby said. The colonel nodded agreement.

'Ranching is a risky business at all times, Kirby. You know that. Next year could be dry again. I have to make a profit while I can.'

'You have a plan,' Kirby prompted.

Tremaine shook his head. 'Down south. Down in Mexico they had a drought year. Terrible times. Their cattle are gaunted out, those that they haven't lost.'

He leaned forward, forearms on the table. His gray-blue eyes grew intent.

'I have a friend down there, a good man. Don Honario Trujillo-Lopez. You wouldn't know him. It was after you left the Rangers that we met. He and I worked both sides of the border fighting Comanches. We correspond from time to time.

'Anyway. Don Trujillo-Lopez has a thousand head of cattle he can't feed: I have the graze.'

'You want to drive them north.'

'Exactly. I can fatten them up over spring and early summer. Drive them to Kansas and turn a hell of a good profit.'

'It's a good plan.'

Tremaine was a cautious man at heart. He was not planning on breeding the Mexican cattle and keeping them on the land indefinitely. Then if he had another dry year he'd find himself in the same position as his Mexican friend.

'I want you with me, Kirby.'

'Of course, sir.'

'I've collected a dozen men to help with the drive. Some of them are good. Some I have doubts about.'

'Like your ramrod?'

'Exactly. Asa Donahue keeps the others in line around here. He's been useful up to now. He brought four men in with him.' Tremaine rose, opened a small window over his zinc sink and looked out at his promising land.

'Good men are hard to find out here, Kirby. Putting together a decent crew is just about the most difficult

11

thing there is to do on a ranch. But they are fighting men, and we will need them.'

'Yes?' Kirby's eyes grew curious.

'The Comancheros. They're still roaming the country between here and Mexico, and in force. Rapacious, without morals – well, you know how they are.'

'All too well,' Kirby reflected. Bands of ex-Confederates, Indians who had jumped their reservations out of frustration, revolutionary Mexicans, former slaves all thrown together for one cause – to plunder as much as they could, without a scruple among them. They were an army of their own, a roving, pillaging army.

'I can better understand why you took on people like Asa,' Kirby said.

'Yes.' Tremaine turned back from the window and leaned against the sink, arms folded. 'But how far can I trust them, Kirby? Any more than the Comancheros? I hadn't met a single one of my new crew before I took them on, except Tomas – you'll meet him later.'

'I see. My job, then is . . . ?'

'Is to help me drive those cattle northward. And,' Tremaine added significantly, 'to watch my back.'

'Do you think they want the cattle?'

'That could be. They could have designs on the herd, yes.'

Kirby understood. A thousand head of cattle on the hoof, even in poor condition, represented a lot of money. If something should befall Colonel Tremaine on the trail back, who would know? They could kill the colonel, bury his body, appropriate the bill of sale from Trujillo-Lopez and sell them at the first opportunity with no questions asked. *If* they were that kind of men.

Kirby asked the Colonel, 'Have you any reason to think

they have designs on the herd?'

'None. None at all. Kirby, I have been around hard men all of my life. I'll give them the benefit of the doubt, partly because I am desperate for hands right now.'

He smiled very thinly. 'But that does not mean I trust them. I have my pension, everything I've worked for all my life tied up in this ranch, and I've borrowed against it, gambled, you'd have to say, everything on bringing the herd through.'

'I understand.'

'I can't guarantee you much, Kirby, little but a long trail and a percentage of the profits once we've brought the herd home and get them fattened for market.'

'I'm not asking for anything more,' Kirby McBride said.

'I don't want you to feel like a hired gun.'

It was Kirby's turn to smile. 'Nothing is further from my mind, sir. I feel like a man who is offering to pitch in on a tough job for a friend. And,' he added, 'for the old Ranger who saved a young green comrade's life at Anchor Wells.'

'As long as you understand, Kirby. If we don't get through there's nothing at all I can pay you with.'

'I understand.' Kirby looked down at the empty coffee cup he held between his hands. Silent for a moment, he then asked, 'What about Asa Donahue? How do you expect him to react to this?'

'Why, Kirby,' the colonel said, 'I suppose he'll try to make sure you don't last out the day on this job.'

The colonel's eyes shifted. The door had opened and a silent figure had entered, a soft-footed, slender man.

'Oh, Tomas, come on in.'

'I did not wish to disturb you,' a soft Spanish voice replied.

'It's all right. We were just about through. Tomas, this is Kirby McBride. He is the new *jefe*, understand?'

'Of course,' the man replied, in a voice like a purr. He came out of the shadows and Kirby could now make out a wiry man, silver-stitched black sombrero in hand, crossed gunbelts worn low on his slender hips. He was dressed in faded black jeans and a blue shirt. His clothes were old, but he gave the impression of being a man once used to much finer things.

'Tomas is the only man you can trust completely, Kirby.' To Tomas he said simply, 'Kirby's orders are mine, understand, Tomas?'

'As you say, *patron*,' the young Mexican agreed with a broad smile that showed one gold tooth.

No further explanations were given, but from Tomas's manner it seemed that more than one man owed Colonel Tremaine a debt that would never be forgotten. All that mattered to Kirby was that the colonel trusted Tomas implicitly, therefore Kirby knew that he, too, could trust the young *vaquero*.

'Please show Kirby where he will sleep, Tomas,' Tremaine said, and now there was a touch of weariness in his voice. 'I must see to my horse.'

'It has been done, *señor*,' Tomas replied.

'Thank you. Thank you both. Now if you will excuse me. . . .'

'Of course,' both of the younger men answered almost in unison, and Kirby rose to leave. The weariness he thought he had detected in Tremaine's voice had been confirmed. He was tired, very tired, and Kirby wondered suddenly if the colonel was as robust as he would have people believe. Could he be ill, or simply exhausted? Either of these could explain his reason for searching out his old Texas Ranger comrade to assist him with the trail drive.

14

Kirby followed Tomas to the door. The two put on their hats again and stood for a minute on the covered porch, looking out across the long land and to the skies where white clouds were gathering now, cutting out the sun. The wind had decreased, but far away to the north distant thunder rumbled like an omen of trouble on the way.

And trouble wasn't long in arriving.

TWO

Kirby McBride's bunk was in a small room by itself at the north end of the bunkhouse. A plank door separated him from the rest of the crew. The bunk was of poles with a lattice of rawhide straps supporting a thin tick mattress. The wind slithered through the chinks in the log walls and rendered the two thin army blankets Kirby had virtually useless. But he had slept in worse places, and it was relatively comfortable.

Outside, the wind, vacillating between a teasing breeze and a gusting menace, drove rain down across the valley. The thunder, distant at times, startlingly close at others, followed on the heels of intimidating displays of white, forked lightning. Sometimes the bunkhouse shook with the power of the storm, at others the rain had a nearly lulling effect. Especially, Kirby reflected, for a man who was under a roof for the first time in a week and a half.

Beyond the heavy door he could still occasionally hear the sounds of the cowhands playing cards. Light bled through the cracks in the door from their smoky kerosene lantern. He could smell the smoke from their pipes and catch a whiff of whiskey – always forbidden but inevitably present.

Nevertheless he slept in relative comfort.

It wasn't until long after midnight when the night was dreadfully cold and suddenly, almost eerily silent, that Asa Donahue made his move.

The door, latched with only a thin one-by-two-inch drawbar was booted open and it slammed against the wall as Asa burst through. Kirby, instantly awake, saw the silhouette of the big man, and behind him, illuminated only by starlight, three or four other cowboys.

Kirby reached for his holstered Colt hanging on his bedpost, but he was too slow. Asa lurched across the small room and slammed his boot into Kirby's wrist. Even by that dim light Kirby could see Asa's triumphant grin.

'Time to move on, cowboy,' Asa said.

Kirby tried to come to his feet and caught a fist to his jaw for his trouble. His head snapped back as Asa chuckled. Three more right-hand shots followed, two into Kirby's ribs, one glancing off his skull as he barely managed to turn his face aside.

He rolled from the bunk and onto the floor. Stunned, Kirby tried to rise, but Asa's knee caught him on the shoulder and drove him down again.

'You're through, McBride, understand?'

Asa hovered so closely over Kirby that he could feel the heat of his body, smell the alcohol and rank tobacco on him.

And he was so near that Kirby's hands were able to shoot out and grab the big man's ankles. He yanked with all of his strength and Asa went off balance. The big man's feet went out from under him and he toppled over backwards, his head slamming into the floor as he fell.

Now the other hands crowded into the doorway, hooting and shouting.

Asa Donahue was quick for a big man, but Kirby

McBride was first to his feet and, as Asa came up, Kirby stuck a straight right into his face, all of the power in his shoulder slamming his fist against Asa's mouth.

Surprised, the big man tottered back, a trickle of dark blood showing at the corner of his mouth. He muttered a curse and took a step forward. And ran right into another stunning blow driven by McBride's powerful arm.

Astonished, off balance, Asa began throwing wild wind-milling punches, which Kirby blocked or ducked away from easily. One of them did catch Kirby on the shoulder, deadening the nerves in his arm briefly, but no permanent damage was done, and Kirby, angry and fully alert now, moved forward deliberately.

He jabbed two straight lefts into Asa's face, and the big man staggered backwards on wobbly legs. The cowboys were silent now, and they began to back away even before Kirby swung a vicious right uppercut into the point of Donahue's chin and the big man's eyes rolled back and his knees buckled.

Asa Donahue hit the ground with a force that shook the bunkhouse floor. Even before he was down, Kirby had swung around and with what seemed amazing speed, slipped his Colt from the holster on the bedpost and cocked it in one smooth motion.

'I don't have another fistfight in me tonight, boys,' he told the hands in the doorway. 'The next one who steps forward is going to take a bullet.' Into the silence that followed he said, 'Now get him out of here.' He toed Asa's unconscious form and two men – one of them Red – took Asa under the arms reluctantly, and with extreme wari-ness, dragged him from the darkened room.

Kirby kicked the door shut behind them and sagged back on his bunk. His ribs ached, his head was pounding, but, as the colonel had told him long ago, 'Never let the enemy know how badly you're hurt. He just might decide to come back.'

He leaned back and waited out the rest of the night, Colt revolver in hand, listening to the fitful storm.

Sometime shortly before dawn Kirby must have dozed off because when he awoke the sun was bright and by the time he pulled on his boots and went out into the bunkhouse it was deserted except for one old man who sat in the corner mending a piece of broken harness. The old man's eyes lifted cautiously. Neither of them said a word, only a meaningless nod of greeting passing between them, and Kirby walked out onto the bunkhouse steps, feeling stiff and raw, ribs still throbbing with dull pain.

The sky had cleared. The few drifting clouds off toward the horizon were spattered with the pink of dawn on their undersides. The corral was empty, the yard silent except for the rhythmic ringing of the blacksmith's hammer in his shed.

Tomas was sitting cross-legged on the end of the porch, weaving a *reata* of strips of new leather. He looked up from under his black sombrero and smiled.

' 'Morning, boss.'

' 'Morning. Is the colonel up?'

'He rode out an hour ago.' Tomas rose from his position with catlike grace. 'He's still looking for a few more horses to buy. Long drive, we will need fresh mounts.'

'The men. . . ?' Kirby asked, looking around the deserted yard.

'Here and there,' Tomas smiled, coiling his unfinished *reata*. 'I think mostly they're hiding out.'

'Hiding out?' Kirby said, puzzled.

'To see which way the wind's going to blow this morning,' Tomas explained with a grin. He studied Kirby's face with narrowed eyes and said, 'You don't look like he hardly touched you.'

'It just doesn't show,' Kirby said. So Tomas had heard about the fight already. That wasn't really surprising, he supposed. Tomas waited expectantly as if he wanted Kirby to tell him what had happened, but he was disappointed.

'What's up for today?'

'The colonel, he left a list of things for you to do on the table. Couple of 'em I already took care of.'

'*Gracias.*'

'*Por nada,*' Tomas answered with a shrug. 'I work here, too, boss.'

'Please! Don't call me "boss", Tomas. The name's Kirby.'

'Sure,' Tomas replied with a nod, and the two men walked toward the door of the house. There wasn't much on the list. One tire needed to be replaced on a wagon wheel, but apparently the blacksmith was already at work on that. Round-up a few of the older mares and their colts who wouldn't be traveling to Mexico and pen them up. The old man Kirby had seen in the bunkhouse, Sampson by name, who would be acting as caretaker while they were gone, was going to feed them there for a few days. This was so the horses would not try to follow their herding instinct and follow the rest of them toward Mexico.

The list went on. Pay the men. In advance.

'We might lose a few of them by doing that,' Kirby commented.

'They're no good for this if they're going to run off whenever they take a notion. Besides, the rest of them, it will keep happy on the trail, right?' Tomas pointed out.

'OK. Where's the colonel keep the gold?'

Tomas grinned and unbuttoned his shirt. He withdrew a small chamois sack and tossed it onto the table. So then – that was just *how* much the colonel trusted the *vaquero*. And Kirby!

'We'll do that when they come in for dinner, all right?'

There were a couple of other small matters such as handing out extra ammunition and making sure every man had a spare blanket in his bedroll. Beyond that it seemed that the colonel and Tomas had taken care of all the incidentals necessary to a long trail drive.

'There's not really that much food here,' Kirby did say, as the two men examined the larder.

'Enough for the trail down. For the drive back, Don Trujillo-Lopez will provision us.'

'Do you know the trail well, Tomas?' Kirby wanted to know.

'Me?' Tomas smiled. 'Since I was a boy I have known it.'

'Good. I was thinking . . .' He was thinking that the colonel had not looked well the day before. If something happened to Tremaine there could be a problem. Actually, he wondered if the colonel was wise to make the trip at all, even knowing how very important it was to him.

'All right,' Kirby said, closing the larder door, folding the list of instructions and tucking it away in his pocket. 'Let's get to it and see what we can accomplish this morning.' He paused. 'For the record, Tomas – what is your last name?'

'Me?' The young man grinned broadly. 'I thought you knew that, Kirby. I thought the colonel he has told you. My full name is Tomas Trujillo-Lopez.'

And Kirby wasn't sure if that explained a lot of things . . . or just presented more questions to be answered.

*

Kirby decided to saddle his horse and go out on his own looking for some of the mares and colts, the older horses who would not be going with them on the trail drive, and start bringing them in. He could have probably gathered a few of the crew, but he doubted they would work well for him; besides, he wanted to be alone for awhile.

As he walked across the ranch yard, muddy from last night's rain, he passed a lanky blond cowboy he had not seen before. The man appeared indolent, cocksure, quite pleased with himself and the world at large. He was leaning against the corral, bootheel hooked on the low rail, chewing on a matchstick. He spoke softly as Kirby walked past, glancing at him.

'He's in there,' the blond cowboy said.

'Who?'

'Asa.' The cowboy pointed toward the stable with his matchstick. 'I saw him go in a little while ago. He's alone.'

'Thanks,' Kirby nodded.

'Thought you might want to know,' the cowboy said, and he went back to what he had been doing before – that is, nothing at all.

Kirby shifted his gunbelt almost imperceptibly and continued on, angling toward the stable, the door of which stood only partially open. His senses, on the alert now after the cowboy's warning, seemed to take in everything at once, the wind-ruffled oaks, the silver drifting clouds, a distant crow wheeling through the air.

He paused only briefly at the stable door. Toeing it open he entered and moved sharply to his left three paces.

Asa was standing there unmoving, between the rows of stalls. His thumbs were hooked in his belt. Kirby waited for the man to make a move toward his gun, but Asa did not try it.

'What is it, Asa?'

'Take it easy, McBride. Don't go getting gun happy on me.' Asa lifted his hands slowly to shoulder height where he held them. 'I just wanted to ask you something.'

'Such as?' Kirby asked suspiciously. There was a bruise on the big man's jaw from their scuffle the night before. Asa stood there glowering, but not, apparently wanting a fight.

'After last night . . .' Asa said, coming forward a few steps. 'I just wanted to know if I'm being fired.'

Kirby hadn't considered that. Now he turned it over rapidly in his mind. They couldn't afford to lose any hands. And Asa had brought four men in with him. They might decide to follow him back out. That would leave them destitute of hands for the long drive, and they were ready to start for Mexico now. Besides, any firing was to be done by the colonel, he decided. *He* must have heard of it already if Tomas knew.

'It's not my place to fire you, Asa,' Kirby said. 'And if I'm asked, I'll tell the Colonel I think we should keep you on.'

Asa relaxed fractionally. His hands lowered to belt level again.

He smiled crookedly, 'Good. No sense in letting a fist-fight ruin things for all of us, is there? It was just one of those things – I was sore about having you replace me.'

I'll bet you were, Kirby thought. Especially if it was true that he and his men had designs on the Mexican herd and possibly the ranch itself. No, there was still no trusting Asa Donahue.

Kirby said, 'We'll forget it for now. We need every man we have.'

Asa looked as if that was the answer he had expected all along. A sneer lifted the corner of his mouth. He tried unconvincingly to alter it into a friendly smile.

'Then we understand each other?'

'Yes,' Kirby said, 'I think we do.'

Asa nodded and walked past Kirby, keeping his distance as he passed.

When Donahue was gone, Kirby saddled the gray and led him out into the cool sunshine. He rode through the grove of big oak trees, circling the small lake hidden behind them, and started away into the green hills, alert for sign of the mares and their colts.

He hadn't ridden far before he realized he was being followed. Some sixth sense triggered the feeling in the back of his mind. He had been long in wild country where a man's instincts play a part in keeping him alive.

He did not turn in the saddle to look, but kept on, riding down into a shallow depression just deep enough to conceal a man on horseback. Then he yanked the gray's head around and rode swiftly northward, coming up out of the hollow a quarter of a mile on, circling back along the flats. He had been right. Looking at the long grass he could see two distinct trails where the grass had been flattened. One of the trails was his, the other belonged to whoever was following him. He pulled his Winchester from its scabbard and started on more slowly, returning to the gully. He found the blond cowboy there, sitting a leggy sorrel pony with a white blaze and three white stockings, looking slightly puzzled as he glanced up at Kirby's approach.

'There you are,' the blond said affably. 'I wondered where you'd got to.'

'Do you need something?' Kirby asked. His rifle, loosely

held, was still in his free hand.

'I just figured you might want some help. Or some company,' the cowhand said. 'I ain't any good at yardwork. I don't chop wood; I don't fork hay; I don't swamp out barns. What I do is work with this little cutter of mine,' he said, patting the sorrel's neck. 'Cattle, horses, anything that jumps, Fargo and I can get a lasso on.'

Kirby slowly replaced his rifle in its scabbard and nodded. He had to trust *somebody*, didn't he?

'OK, come along. Have you got an idea where the mares might be?'

'Not really. I did see one of them with her colt over south yesterday. Colt didn't look to be more than two weeks old. I figure she's still trying to hide it out.'

Slowly then, the two men started in that direction. The breeze was still cool, but the sun was warm on Kirby's back. The gray moved beneath him easily, its long stride causing its hoofs to sing through the young green grass.

'What'd you say your name was?' Kirby asked, as the two men rode side by side.

'Dallas,' the blond man answered.

'Dallas. . . ?'

'That's all. Just Dallas.'

Kirby shrugged. There were a lot of men out West who had no last names for various reasons. Things done in their past. So you met many a man called 'Slim' or 'Tex' or even just 'Kid somebody'. It wasn't unusual in this part of the country and a man didn't pry if he was wise.

Looking him over, Kirby took in the lines and gait of the sorrel Dallas rode. A horse like that was worth a small fortune. High-stepping, deep-chested, but light in the legs. The sort of animal only a rich man – and sometimes outlaws – rode. Quick out of the gate. The horse's trappings weren't fancy, nor was the saddle Dallas sat so easily. His gun was another matter.

It, too, was not the sort of sidearm many working cowboys wore or could afford. Staghorn grips, slick blue-ing, riding in a holster that was cut low where the index fmger would settle. Kirby had seen many a cowboy whose sidearm, worn through hard weather, was rusted nearly to the point of being unusable, worn only because everyone wore a gun.

Dallas was not that sort either.

Curious but silent, Kirby rode on, squinting into the sun, searching for the mare and her colt.

'Know anything about them Comancheros?' Dallas asked lazily after awhile.

'Some. Why?'

'Just wondered. Thought you might. I hear the band roaming around here is the bunch that burned out a family in Big Bend. They say they burned the place down, then killed a woman and her two children for no reason.'

'I heard of that raid. Pointless, wasn't it? I mean there was nothing for them to gain by it.'

'Not a thing,' Dallas agreed.

'What brought that up?' Kirby asked. 'You worried about the Comancheros?'

'Not much,' Dallas said, with a soft smile. 'Maybe they ought to be worried about me, though. They're one reason I chose to ride with the colonel. He's concerned they might hit us. Me,' Dallas said, 'I'm kinda hoping they will. That was my family over in Big Bend, Kirby.'

There was little to be said in response to that. Fortunately at that moment they saw the roan mare and her leggy young colt ahead of them a quarter of a mile or so and Kirby pointed that way and lifted the gray into a canter, riding toward them across the lush grass of the long valley.

Asa and his cronies, Red and Len Parker, were gathered around the corral just then. The colonel had returned with a string of three tough-looking mustangs purchased from a neighbor for the drive, and they were looking the animals over.

'Look who's coming,' Len said, and Asa lifted his eyes.

Dallas and Kirby McBride were riding in, driving two mares and two skittish colts before them.

Red asked, 'Did he buy into your game?'

Asa smiled. 'Sure – I knew they couldn't afford to let us go just now. What else could he do but keep us on?'

'I don't like him cozying up with that Dallas,' Len commented.

Neither did Asa Donahue. Dallas they had marked as a dangerous man the first time they laid eyes on him. A loner, he wore his gun in a way that signified trouble. Where he had drifted in from no one knew but the colonel. Maybe even he didn't know. Dallas had been Asa's primary concern before Kirby McBride had appeared on the scene.

'Accidents can happen to two as well as one,' Asa commented. 'It's a long trail.' He cautioned them, 'Not on the trail down, though. We need them as much as they need us. A thousand head of cattle and the hills full of Comancheros.'

Len nodded his understanding. Once back across the border when they were relaxed, confident. That would be soon enough for any 'accidents'.

Red didn't agree. He had already had a run-in with Dallas and the blond cowboy had humilated him, backing

Red down when gunplay was threatened. Red hadn't had the heart to try his hand, not face to face with the cool-looking, confident Dallas. For now, however, he kept his mouth shut and just watched with the rest of them as Tomas swung open the corral gate and Kirby and Dallas, on that sharp-looking little cutting horse of his, hazed the mares and colts into the pen.

The horses in, Tomas caught up with Kirby. 'The colonel's back. He wants to see you.'

'OK, thanks.'

Dallas who was sitting his horse, leg hooked around the pommel of his saddle as if he were relaxing in an easy chair, nodded a goodbye, swung gracefully to the ground and started toward the stable, the sorrel still tossing its head as if it had just started to warm to its work and was eager for more.

Asa's eyes followed Dallas and then switched to Kirby as he walked the gray horse toward the hitching rail in front of the house.

He wasn't able to decide which one he wanted to kill first.

'Come in,' the colonel's resonant voice called and, as Kirby entered, he added, 'Kirby! Hell, boy, you don't have to knock on my door to come in.'

'That's the way my mother raised me, sir,' Kirby said.

With a pleasant weariness from a decent day's work in his bones, Kirby sagged into a chair, tilted back and said, 'Tomas said you wanted to see me.'

'Yes. Did you see those three new mustangs?'

'I did.'

'I got them for a song. I felt bad about it, but Kimble over at Double E has a baby on the way and another that's sick. I gave him fifty bucks apiece and free graze for his steers on my land while we're gone.'

Kirby smiled. The colonel might have claimed other-wise, but fifty dollars apiece for three half-broken mustangs wasn't unreasonable, and free graze for a man with poor land and little water more than compensated for any inequity.

'Have you paid the men yet, Kirby?'

'I spread the word it would be at dinner-time. We can hand out the extra ammunition and spare blankets at the same time,' Kirby said.

The colonel nodded. 'Then I guess we're ready, Kirby. Tomorrow,' he said, with just a slight furrow of worry on his brow, 'south to Mexico and Vista del Luna.'

'All right, we're as prepared as we're going to get,' Kirby said.

'I suppose so. I wish we had just a couple more trust-worthy men. . . .'

'You've got Tomas. And Dallas – I spent some time with him today. You can count on him, I think.'

'So do I,' the colonel agreed. 'Did he tell you why he signed on?'

'Enough.'

'Yes. I don't like to tell stories out of school, but if he's told you . . .' The colonel shook his head heavily. 'He's got his own agenda. I hope it doesn't get in the way of the job at hand.'

'I didn't get that impression of the man. He'll ride for the brand, I think.'

'I hope so.' The colonel was now noticeably worried. The lines in his face seemed deeper in the shadows. After all, he was risking everything he owned on the success of the drive north.

'I do hope so,' the colonel said again, still thinking

about Dallas apparently. 'We will need a man of his caliber with us. If we do run into Oso . . .'

'*Oso?*'

'The name the Comanchero leader goes by. I'm afraid Dallas might take a notion to do something crazy on his own. The man has no fear, you know. And to have found his wife and children murdered . . .'

'He'll stick,' Kirby said, with more conviction than he felt. After all, every man must have his own agenda, his own plans. Riding for the brand was a code of honor in the West, a loyalty as strong as that the feudal lords expected and received without question. But Dallas was seeking revenge for his lost family, and that involved a different, perhaps stronger sort of honor.

'Who else can I trust, really trust?' Kirby asked.

'Tomas, beyond question. Bull Schultz – you haven't met him yet. After that . . .' Colonel Tremaine spread his hands helplessly. He added no more names to the list.

Asa and his men made up the crew after that. There were two others who had just ridden in. Drifters who had heard there was work here. Two brothers named Tom and Avery, whiskered, laconic Kentuckians the colonel knew nothing about except that they were available.

'Kirby,' the colonel said, 'this is all pretty much on your shoulders, you know. I needed you, son, that's why you're here. Outside of Tomas . . .'

'I understand, sir,' Kirby said quickly.

And he did. Outside of Tomas, there was no one but him the colonel could count on fully.

And very probably Kirby McBride was already marked for death.

THREE

Kirby's sleep was untroubled that night. The nightly poker game had even been abandoned in the bunkhouse, Every man knew he had to be well rested in the morning for the long drive to Mexico.

The yard was a scene of organized confusion when Kirby walked out into the chill of pre-dawn. The wagon was still in the process of being loaded with supplies. Coffee, sugar, flour, bandages among other things. The wranglers – the Peck brothers – had bridled and saddled the lead ponies. The second string, those that would be used to spell the others when needed, were stamping the frost from their hoofs in the corral as they were tied to lead ropes. Last-minute instructions were shouted. Breath steamed from the lips of men and from the flanks of the horses. Ice crackled underfoot as Kirby walked across the yard, glancing toward the eastern horizon, still seeing no sign of approaching dawn. The stars hung heavy and brittle in a clear, cold sky.

He met Tomas on his way to the big house. Tomas wore a heavy brown and red-striped serape over his shoulders. His fancy sombrero had given way to a broad-brimmed, plain brown stetson.

'The colonel's up,' Tomas said in a shivery voice. 'I think he was probably up all night, yes?'

'Probably. I wish there were some way to keep him from making this drive.'

'That, my friend,' Tomas said, 'is as likely as stopping the sun from rising this morning.'

'I know it.' Kirby asked then, 'Are all the hands accounted for?'

'Except for Turkey.' Tomas shrugged.

Turkey was a hand Kirby barely knew. But apparently he had taken his pay and ridden off in the night, figuring a week in San Angelo with his pockets full beat two weeks on the Spanish trail.

'Well, we figured on that,' Kirby said. 'At least it was only him that took off.'

Before they had reached the porch of the house, the colonel appeared in the doorway. He wore a long gray coat, carried the old Spencer carbine in his hand. He had his saddle-bags slung over one shoulder. The old man had a clean shave and a steely look in his eyes.

'Grab some coffee, Kirby,' Tremaine said. 'When I see the first color in the sky, we're starting.'

He was as excited as a kid and skittish as a colt, determined as an old bull at once. The colonel had waited a long while for the drive to begin. Now he was about to find out whether his old age would bring a life of leisure or one of dire poverty. He was eager to roll the dice and find out what came up.

Kirby gulped down two cups of coffee. There was a plate of biscuits on the table as well, and he shoved one in his mouth, poked three more into his own saddle-bags and went back out into the yard.

Now there was the faintest hint of color in the sky to the east, a swath of dull crimson over the night-shadowed plains. A horse whickered and tossed its head. Another answered.

Leather creaked as men swung heavily into their saddles. Dallas appeared on his sorrel, leading Kirby's tall gray horse.

'Thanks, Dallas,' Kirby said.

'It's nothing, Kirby,' Dallas shrugged. 'I couldn't sleep last night. I've been up and about since four. I had to be doing something.'

'Eager for the trail?' Kirby asked, double-checking the cinches before swinging aboard.

'Eager,' Dallas said, looking southward, 'just eager.'

At Kirby's questioning look, Dallas said, 'I know I've got a job to do for the colonel, Kirby. Don't worry about it.'

'And a job to take care of for yourself.'

'If I can, yes. If I can,' Dallas said, and the expression on his face grew suddenly cold and hard enough to surprise Kirby. It was an almost wolfish eagerness that he saw there. He understood the man's urge toward revenge against Oso and the Comancheros, but Dallas's true priorities were still unclear.

From the looks of things – the lining of the horses, the determined looks on the men's faces, the wagon starting heavily from the yard, it seemed for all the world like a group of men intent on a single purpose, an army moving out toward one certain objective.

But it was far from that.

Every man rode with his own agenda, Kirby knew. Dallas and his vengeance lust, Asa and his men . . . waiting to steal a herd and commit murder? The handful of other men Kirby really didn't know at all. Riding without apparent obligation except to their pay. Tremaine, desperate to regain solvency and save everything he owned.

The colonel led them out, his head held high as if he were leading his force into battle. He looked much as Kirby remembered him, but things were not the same anymore.

These men rode for no flag, wore no Ranger badges.

If Oso did attack them, how many would stand and fight for the herd of Mexican steers?

Kirby flipped up the collar of his buffalo coat, tugged his hat lower and started the big gray southward toward the border, riding on the skirts of Colonel Tremaine's dreams.

They moved slowly because of the chuck wagon, but steadily southward, all eyes on the hills which began to close in around them. No rider alone ever traveled this route. The Texas Rangers no longer hunted the Comancheros this far west. Chasing Oso was like pursuing Geronimo, or a ghost. Besides, it took the Comancheros no time at all to slip across the border into Mexico and escape their pursuers.

'Were you in the War?' Dallas asked, as they rode side by side through the golden morning sunlight.

Kirby had shed his buffalo coat as the sun rode higher into the sky, and now he was settled in for the long, long ride south.

'Me?' Kirby smiled. 'No. I was only twelve when it broke out. I tried to follow my brothers into the war, but my mother caught me. She said I was the last of the male line and she was damned if she'd have me shot. She pulled me off the mule I was trying to ride away on and took me home by my ear.'

He smiled in reflection. She had been right, of course. Trevor, his oldest brother, a tall, handsome reflection of everything a Southern gentleman aspired to be, was killed at the First Battle of Bull Run. His second brother, Talbert – Tal – had been taken prisoner by the Union forces, escaped, shot down in pursuit, reimprisoned and left to rot away, losing an arm from gangrene. A second escape attempt had been successful, but no one knew where Tal had gone, pursued by the Northern army until war's end.

'How'd you come to know Colonel Tremaine, then?' Dallas asked, interrupting Kirby's brief reverie.

'After the war my family drifted down from Carolina, looking for new land. Mother died. My sister Beth got married and moved off the rock-and-brush ranch we tried to start outside of San Antonio. . . .' Kirby shrugged. 'I pulled up stakes, drifted for a time and then joined the Rangers. McCulloch himself kind of drafted me.'

'They say he was a tough man.'

'The toughest. I was a cocky kid, though. I thought I was a match for anybody. Had a chip on my shoulder after losing most of my family and the ranch. Well . . . put it this way, the Rangers taught me I wasn't as tough as I had thought.'

'And Tremaine?'

'He was my first commanding officer. Two years of fighting Mexicans, Comanches, Kansas raiders. . . . I learned it took a little more than mouth to win a battle.'

'He saved your life, didn't he?'

'I don't talk much about that, but yes he did,' Kirby admitted. 'I was young and dumb. Or,' – he grinned – 'should I say "younger and dumber"? I got myself cut off from the regiment. I had some idea of saving Texas all by myself. I got myself pinned down at a place called Anchor Wells.'

'I know it,' Dallas said. In actuality Anchor Wells was little more than a buffalo wallow south of Fort Stockton, the only place for miles around with water.

'That shows you how green I was,' Kirby said. 'Only water for miles around – well, of course some unwanted company is going to show up.'

'And they did.'

'Comanches. Maybe a dozen of them. It was a band we'd been chasing, a crazy bunch of young warriors who'd even destroyed a Kiowa camp in the area for no reason we could figure out. They had me pinned down . . . man, you don't think they wanted that water! And me and my old Springfield rifle trying to hold them off.'

'The colonel pulled you out?'

'That's the short version, yeah. *Pulled me out* doesn't cover what that man went through fighting the Indians guerilla-style through the night. Him and his Cherokee scout, name of Firesky. He got captured and they killed him. They cut him up slow through the night so that we had to listen to him die bit by bit. . . . Long ago, Dallas, I don't care to tell it all in detail.'

'I understand.'

'Well,' Kirby said, shifting in his saddle, 'I suppose you might, but no one ever understands another man's life completely, do they?'

'No. You're right.'

'OK. Did you have a reason for bringing this all up, Dallas?

'Not really. Just trail talk.' The cowboy yawned. 'And I was wondering just how far you'd go for Colonel Tremaine.'

Kirby didn't have to think about his answer. 'All the way,' he said with conviction.

'Yeah, that's what I thought. See, Kirby, I have been wondering exactly what our strength is. That is, if we do have a run-in with Oso's Comancheros, how many of these men will stand and fight; how many will try to run away?'

'And there's a reason you're wondering this, Dallas?'

'Yeah, Kirby,' Dallas answered quietly. 'There's a reason . . . because they're already following us.'

Easily then, Kirby let his eyes drift to the west where low, crumbling hills, bright where new green grass dusted red soil, filled the view. And at intervals as they rode in near

36

silence with only the creaking of the chuck wagon's wheels and the low voices of the men, he saw now and then the flitting distant shadow of a mounted man.

Dallas said, 'It don't take long for vultures to gather, friend.'

Kirby made no reply. They rode on, his stolid, plodding gray used to long miles and rough travel alongside Dallas's light-trotting cutting horse. It was true, the vultures were out there, slowly gathering, probably wondering if there was enough loot to make an attack on the colonel's crew worthwhile. Undoubtedly their leaders were mentally counting their guns, estimating what little worth a wagonful of supplies could possibly have, weighing the possibility for profit against casualties.

And wondering what the colonel and his men were doing out on the empty prairie.

Kirby felt confident that they would not attack. Not against a dozen men for a few sacks of supplies.

But they were watching now, knowing something was in the works. And they would wait patiently until the time was right, gathering more forces. Secrecy, on the first morning southward, was already a lost illusion.

'Have you figured it out yet?' Red asked, as he rode next to Asa Donahue. 'McBride, that is.'

'It can't be him,' Len Parker said. 'He's too young.'

'No,' Asa agreed. 'There was another man out from Carolina by that name, damnit. Same lean face. Same blue eyes. . . .' Asa glanced back at Kirby again from where they rode fifty feet behind the toiling supply wagon. 'Tal!' he nearly shouted.

'What?' Red asked.

'Tal McBride! Don't you recall now? In Lawrence! He

was town marshal for a while. One-armed man!'

'God, yes,' Red said. 'I remember now.'

'So do I,' Len said bitterly. 'I recall folks back there saying they wished the Yankees had shot off his gun arm instead of leaving him with that quick hand of his.'

'Well,' Red said with relief, 'at least we know he ain't *that* McBride.'

'No,' Asa said. 'He's got both arms – but it makes you wonder, don't it, boys? If they are relatives – brothers is likely – are we riding into something we haven't counted on? Maybe,' Asa said meditatively, 'there's other parties that have designs on the colonel's herd and his ranch. Maybe,' Asa said, 'we ought to do some hard thinking about this.'

'What do you mean?' Len asked, feeling a little uneasy suddenly.

'Kirby is no easy mark, we know that. Why is he cozying up to Dallas? We know what Dallas used to be.'

'They say he gave up the gun and went to sod-busting.'

'Yes, and before that? In Wichita?'

'They say he cut down all three Sabo brothers in a fair fight.'

'And you believe he would give it up to settle with a skirt?' Asa Donahue smirked, as if the idea of a gunman going straight for love was absurd.

'Then,' he went on, 'if that is Tal McBride's brother, boys, we may be running into something we didn't count on at all.'

'You think they're after the same things we are?' Len asked almost in panic.

'I don't know,' Asa answered, stroking his chin. 'All I'm saying is we had better just tread lightly for a time until it all comes clear.'

Three days later with their water barrels low and the

horses salt-flecked and weary, the men dry-mouthed and caked with road dust, they rode onto the Rancho las Luna in Mexico.

The ranch had a spectacular setting with the high eastern mountains rising firm and stark against the sky. Scattered oaks and a few sycamores stood along the creek bottoms. But the creeks, Kirby noticed, were almost dry, only twisting silver rivulets wandering aimlessly across the yellow grass valley. There were cattle, many of them, everywhere. Longhorns, they were of course, gaunt and angry looking. They would be cantankerous and mean on a long drive, unwilling to leave the home range and the little water they had. The Texans had their work cut out for them.

The hacienda of Don Trujillo-Lopez was a beautiful two-story white house with Spanish tiles on a sloping roof. Two balconies overhung the arched portico beneath. Dry bougainvillaea vines clung to the trellises with only a few red-violet flowers growing there. Behind the house, in what Kirby assumed to be a courtyard in the Spanish style, two lofty jacaranda trees stood, dry as all else.

Three *vaqueros*, one of them mounted, turned their heads from their private discussion to watch the Americans ride in. Tremaine drew up his horse.

'Hold the men back, Donahue,' the colonel said. 'Set up camp in the oaks by the creek.'

'All right,' Asa said, as if this were a personal affront.

'Water the horses and spread your bedrolls. I'll try to have some food sent out to you. Kirby, come along with me.' Tomas, of course, went along without being invited. It was, after all, his father's house.

The three men rode past the watching *vaqueros* silently. Tremaine removed his hat in a sign of greeting. Oddly, Kirby noted, none of the men spoke to Tomas although he must have known them. It was a strange sort of homecoming for the young Mexican. No greetings, cries of joy . . . only dark eyes following them across the dusty yard to the front of the hacienda. The tall man with the silver hair dressed in immaculate white linen stepped out to meet them.

'Lopez!' Tremaine called out with genuine affection.

'Tremaine,' the Mexican answered with equal enthusiasm. 'Step down, my friend, come into my *casa*. It has been a long trail, I know.'

'Long and dusty. Seeing you is like a cool drink of water,' the colonel said floridly.

The Mexican's eyes went to Kirby, their expression giving nothing away. Then Lopez looked at his son. If anything, the inspection was even briefer, bordering, in fact, on dismissal.

Tomas shrugged to Kirby and said, 'So you see, the prodigal son is not always welcomed warmly.'

Kirby said nothing. He knew nothing of the circumstances under which Tomas and his father had parted company. He just swung down tiredly, loosening the double cinches of his saddle while the two older men embraced warmly.

'Now, please do come in out of the sun,' Don Trujillo-Lopez said with his arm over the colonel's shoulders; 'all of you,' he added after a moment.

Dusting off the best he could, Kirby trailed them into the coolness of the big house. And just for a moment before he entered he caught a glimpse of the young, dark-eyed girl in yellow on the balcony above them.

They entered along a tiled corridor. The walls were paneled with dark wood. The ceiling was high, heavily beamed. Crossing a massively furnished front room they entered a formal dining-room. The table and chairs were dark, hand-carved in the Spanish style. The chairs were high-backed, the cushions covered in purple velvet. A candelabra of ornate silver rested in the center of the table. As the men sat to the table a small, shy Indian servant of middle years appeared and, at a signal from Lopez, scurried away again, returning in minutes with a pitcher of cool water, a tray of sweets and a carafe of pale wine.

'To business,' Don Trujillo-Lopez said almost immediately. 'It is not our way to hurry things like this, as you know, Tremaine, but time is of the essence these days.'

'I understand.'

'I wonder if you do,' the Mexican said with a frown. 'I can no longer pay my men. If not for you I would have been forced to simply shoot my cattle for hides. They are not content to stay on the rancho, the grass has grown so poor. The men must fight constantly to contain them. If they were not loyal to a man to me . . .'

'As you say,' Tremaine said soothingly, 'at times expediency is called for. Tomas?'

Tomas nodded and, unbuttoning his shirt, removed the rawhide sack he wore on a thong around his neck. The gold coins in the sack clinked as he placed it on the table and pushed it toward his father.

The don, Kirby could not help but notice, had still not said a single word to his son.

'These matters . . .' the don said, genuinely embarrassed. It was not the way he would have chosen to do business, especially with an old friend. In normal times there would have been a feast, a fandango perhaps with dancing and conversations about matters other than those of business. But these were not good times.

'I have now only about eight-hundred head of steers that are trail-worthy,' the Mexican said without touching the sack of gold. 'Those who are ill or weak have been culled. There will be enough grass and water for those who remain. My *vaqueros*, of course, are at your disposal to help you round up the others.'

'Of course.'

Hesitantly then, the proud don opened the gold sack and stacked the twenty- and fifty-dollar pieces into neat columns.

From somewhere a second servant, an old man, appeared. In his hand was a carefully hand-written contract on parchment.

'I have already signed this, Tremaine. The terms we have already agreed to.'

Tremaine nodded. He didn't even glance at the bill of sale. A man's word meant so much more than a piece of paper to men like these in those times.

'There is one matter we have not discussed,' Lopez said. Shoveling the gold back in the pouch, handing it to his manservant. 'The safe, Miguel.' The servant bowed and went away with the gold.

'There is one more matter?' Tremaine asked curiously. 'What could that be, Don Lopez?'

'Something that has arisen.' The Mexican fumbled for the right words. 'I wish . . . I almost would say: you *must* help me with this matter.'

'Anything at all,' Tremaine agreed quickly.

'It is Angela,' Lopez said and, as he began to speak, the girl in the yellow dress emerged from the shadows, her eyes downcast, her dark hair shiny and carefully held in place with a high Spanish comb, her body lithe and still just a little boyish.

'. . . She must travel with you.'

FOUR

Kirby and the colonel exchanged incredulous glances. Surely Don Lopez knew that what he was proposing was crazy: escort a young woman across Comanchero country, a hard land with a rough crowd of men.

Tremaine said cautiously, 'I know I said I would do anything for you, Lopez, but what you are asking is incredible. Impossible.'

'It must be done,' Don Lopez said solemnly.

'I cannot understand you. Why must this be done?' Tremaine spread his hands. Kirby watched the girl from the corner of his eyes. She walked slowly, gracefully, before the large window, the late sunlight silhouetting her slender figure.

'It is Escobar!' Tomas burst out angrily. His father's eyes slashed at him. 'I knew it all along. I knew it would come to this!'

'Silence!'

'Silence?' Tomas laughed. 'That is what you instructed me before – and now it has come to this. You . . . afraid of Escobar!'

'I command you to be silent,' Don Trujillo-Lopez said. His fist suddenly banged down against the heavy table. To Tremaine, he said, 'I beg your forgiveness for my behavior.'

'It is nothing,' the colonel replied, his eyes still narrowed in puzzlement.

'My son is right,' the don said, as if it pained him to admit it. He ran a hand over his silver hair and half-smiled bitterly. 'Luis Escobar is the son of my closest friend here. They own the neighboring rancho. Now his father is very ill and Luis has grown arrogant and threatening. Unfortunately . . . in the hard times, I was forced to borrow some money from him.'

'And in return all he wants is my sister!' Tomas said wildly. This time his father did not attempt to silence him.

Angela had turned from the window to face them, but still she said nothing.

'But why send her with me?' Tremaine asked, still not understanding.

'I am ashamed to admit it, but I cannot stand alone against the man,' Lopez said. 'Angela has an aunt in San Antonio. If she goes there, she will be safely away. She can complete her education. If she remains here longer . . .'

'Luis Escobar is a madman,' Tomas said, and now his father only sighed as he listened to his son. 'I tried to tell you, Father!'

'I know, I know, Tomas. I thought you were jealous of the man. I believed you were making trouble with my old friend over nothing. I didn't—'

'You never saw the way he looked at Angela? Like a hungry wolf.'

'Please, Tomas.' Lopez was silent for a long time before he met his son's gaze. 'I was wrong. This is not easy for me to admit. I was wrong about all of it.'

'Still,' Kirby put in without being invited, 'there must be some better way of sending the girl north. With a rough crew like we've got – and Oso out there.'

'That is precisely it, Mr. McBride. Oso is out there. Escobar would think nothing of overpowering a few of my *vaqueros* if that was what it took, assuming I could spare them just now. What is needed is a large body of men – perhaps even rough men are needed – to guard her on her way north.'

Tremaine was staring at his fingertips meditatively. Kirby knew what was going on in his mind. With all of the other problems the long drive promised, why this? And yet, how could he refuse his old friend?

The colonel asked, 'Will this Escobar try to follow her?'

'I fear so, yes.'

'He will,' Tomas said firmly. 'He feels Angela is his due since he has loaned Father money. I know the man. He is a snake.'

'I have asked him to wait,' Don Lopez said, rubbing his forehead. 'For payment. I knew you would not fail me, old friend. But now he has refused payment even. "It is too late", is what he has said. "We must merge our holdings through marriage." I am afraid, as my son says, he is a snake. There is nothing to be said to him. If his father were well . . . but he is not. He is gravely ill and when I spoke to him, I am afraid he did not understand me. Or even know who I was.'

Tremaine sighed, made a loose gesture with one hand, looked again at the girl before the window and at the worried face of his old friend. There was no way to refuse. There must be honor in friendship as well.

'Have the girl's trunks packed,' Tremaine said.

Angela scurried away, holding her skirts off the floor. Her face was glowing, but Kirby could not tell if it was from pleasure or from the terrible excitement of the moment. While the two older men spoke of old times, Tomas and Kirby went out onto the porch of the hacienda. Doves winged homeward across the sundown sky and an owl hooted from the shelter of the oak grove.

'This Escobar,' Kirby asked, 'is he really that dangerous?'

'Yes,' Tomas answered softly, 'very dangerous, Kirby.'

'That's the whole reason behind you leaving home? You thought Escobar wanted your sister and your father wouldn't listen to you?'

'You do not understand, Kirby. In my country a man does not speak out against his father. When we disagreed it was the same as challenging his authority.'

'I see.'

'Perhaps you do. I think not entirely.'

'No, I guess not. I'll tell you, though, I don't think much of this plan of your father's. Taking your sister north with us.' Kirby shook his head. 'It won't be easy for her.'

'It would be worse for her to remain here, believe me.'

'I guess I'll have to take your word for it.'

'My father is no longer young, Kirby. He has few *vaqueros* anymore. The rancho is dying, and so I am afraid . . . is he. There will be nothing left for Angela here soon. No money, no men to watch out for her . . . and, perhaps, I fear . . . not even her father.'

'Sorry,' was all Kirby could think of to say. He still liked none of this, but he could see what life would become for an unprotected, destitute girl on a dying ranch if anything did happen to Don Lopez, and Tomas seemed to believe that end was in sight.

They spoke for a little while longer and then Kirby rode over to the camp the Texans had set up in the oak grove. The narrow creek running through it caught the early starlight and gleamed silver as it wove its way through the trees. Someone was playing a harmonica. Mostly the camp was quiet. The men were trail-weary, not up to jokes and games.

Big Bull Schultz to whom Kirby had only spoken in passing sauntered across as he swung down from the gray horse, his bear-like shoulders rolling.

'Everything set, Kirby?'

'Far as I know. Money's changed hands. Tomorrow we'll start bunching the herd.'

'Gonna be hell trying to work with those nasty old longhorns.' Bull took off his hat and scratched his head.

'It will,' Kirby agreed. Then he grinned, 'That's what we're being paid for, though, isn't it?'

'Yeah, it is. That doesn't mean I have to like it, though.'

There was a lot Kirby didn't like about this drive either, but he had signed on for it, and that was that.

The Comancheros would be watching, probably smiling, as they watched the Texans doing their hard work for them. They would not strike until the colonel's drive was well underway and the herd trail-broken. Nor, for that matter, would Asa Donahue – if taking the herd was his plan, and Kirby was almost certain that it was.

Add to that the girl, Angela, and her unwanted suitor, Escobar, and it didn't make a good mix at all.

Not at all.

Kirby took his bedroll to a huge, bowed old sycamore a little distant from the others and spread it out under the tree to watch the night sky roll over for a time before he closed his eyes and slept deeply.

It was Dallas who awoke him just before dawn.

'All right, Kirby, it's time. Let's collect us some cows.'

Yawning, Kirby McBride sat up and rubbed his head for a minute, letting the fog of sleep clear away. Then he made up his bedroll and walked to the creek to splash cold water on his face and head.

Kirby decided to give the gray horse the day off. It was

a long-striding animal, easy on a rider, but he was too big and bulky to be a cowpony. Kirby had been alternating on the ride down, using a stubby little buckskin with a black mane and tail. Balky in the morning, nevertheless he was a clever little horse and Kirby decided to saddle the buckskin for this morning's work.

After a sullen breakfast the men rode to meet the half-dozen *vaqueros* Lopez had sent to work with them and guide them around the rancho. Neither side seemed to like the other much, but that didn't matter as long as the job got done.

'There is a narrow canyon,' Tomas told Kirby, 'not exactly a box canyon, but very narrow at the south end. The *vaqueros* will throw a brush fence across that. We should be able to hold the cattle there for at least a day or two.'

'Sounds good,' Kirby agreed.

'And the *vaqueros* have already rounded up maybe half of the steers. We can concentrate on the strays – and there are many.'

Kirby nodded. He wasn't really looking forward to this. Trying to prod an angry longhorn from the brush was inviting a swipe of those menacing horns. Hopefully they could get the cattle massed without a man or horse being seriously injured.

He and Dallas met, and by mutual if unspoken agreement they began working the broken land of the south-western quarter together. Arroyos carved into the dry plain, some heavy brush to the far south, made for many hiding places for the range-tough steers.

Before lunch they had managed to drag, prod and frighten two dozen steers toward the canyon where two *vaqueros* hied them in with the others.

Riding alone early that afternoon, Kirby ran into Luis

Escobar for the first time.

Kirby was sitting on the brow of a dry grass, brush-clotted hill, his hat on the pommel of his saddle, eyes searching the tangle of hills for stray longhorns.

He knew immediately that it had to be Luis Escobar riding toward him, sitting that tall black horse with the white tail and a splash of white on its flank. The silver trappings of his bridle and saddle glinted in the sunlight. Two men rode beside him, both wearing huge, wind-folded sombreros. They rode directly toward Kirby.

'What are you doing here?' Escobar demanded, as they halted before him. Luis Escobar was a handsome man with a thin black mustache and cold eyes. He knew he was good-looking and had the insolence to match his looks.

'I asked you . . .'

'Round-up for Don Trujillo-Lopez,' Kirby said quietly. He put his hat back on and shifted a little in his saddle, his right hand dropping nearer his gun as he lowered it.

'You are on my property,' Escobar said.

'I don't think so. Don Lopez told me his line runs all the way to the butte.'

'You do not understand me,' Escobar said carefully. His men were edging their horses nearer. 'I said you are on my land. I am ordering you off.'

'Friend, if I was on your land, which you know I'm not, I still wouldn't be doing you any harm. I'm looking for Trujillo-Lopez cattle and I can read brands well enough to tell which ones they are.'

'I will give you one minute,' Escobar said, and Kirby didn't think the man was bluffing either. There was a nasty edge to his voice. There was no telling what would have happened then, but a voice from behind Kirby broke in.

'Any trouble here, Kirby?' Dallas asked in a soft drawl,

as he drifted his sorrel out of the head-high brush.

'Not unless he wants there to be.'

Escobar, surprised at Dallas's sudden appearance settled back in his saddle. He didn't like the odds so much now, it seemed.

'You have been warned,' he said, jabbing a finger at Kirby. Then he spun his black horse around and with a last backward glance, he galloped off to the south, his two sidekicks following.

'Nice fella,' Dallas commented drily.

'I think he's a little crazy,' Kirby said on reflection.

Or greedy? Did he want Angela so much or the rancho of his neighbor to add to his own holdings? Through marriage he would have claim to the property of Don Trujillo-Lopez if anything were to happen to the old don. Kirby shrugged it off. It was none of his business so long as the man stayed out of his way.

'Let's get to work, Dallas.'

For the rest of that day and all of the next they combed the hills, pushing the longhorns to their makeshift pen in the narrow canyon. On the evening of the second day, Tremaine and Kirby had a conference.

'What's the count, Kirby?' the colonel asked.

'I make it seven hundred seventy. Give or take. We have a few steers break out now and then. The canyon's getting too crowded to hold them comfortably. A few of them have taken to fighting with each other. They don't much like it in there.'

'We're close enough,' the colonel decided. 'It's to the point where it's costing us more to stay here hunting the odd stray than to start up the trail a few head shy.'

'I agree with you, Colonel.'

'All right,' the old soldier said decisively. 'Have the men

50

who aren't watching the herd turn in early tonight. Make sure those on night herd are relieved and get a chance for a few hours' sleep, too. Tomorrow we're starting north.'

Kirby looked toward the hacienda, dark now against the evening sky. 'What about our guest?'

'She's still going with us,' Tremaine said worriedly. 'I thought Lopez might have second thoughts. I was hoping that he would, but he's determined that Angela be taken away from here.'

'There's been no sign of her friend?'

'Escobar, you mean? No,' the colonel said. 'Which is a little strange to me, having heard what I have of his character. You'd think, Kirby, that he would have ridden in here raising Cain. By now he must have gotten word that she is planning to leave.'

'He'll be along,' Kirby said quietly. 'I've met the man. Sooner or later, he'll be along.'

Tomas thought so, too. Kirby met him on his way back to the camp-fires along the creek. The young man was worried and eager to be away at once.

'I would like to stay here, help my father. What can be done, Kirby? Nothing. I will just try to help the colonel, and my sister now.'

'That's all you can do, I guess. Are you planning on coming back someday, Tomas?' Kirby asked.

'To what?' Tomas looked around at the dry rancho, the dead and dying trees, the big empty house.

'Won't you inherit this?' Kirby asked.

'I don't know. When my father and I were arguing, I said many things I did not mean. I told him I wanted no part of his land and property. I don't know what he wrote in his will after that. Angela, I think, will inherit.'

'Is that what Escobar is counting on, Tomas? Is that why

he wants to marry her?'

'It is not the only reason, Kirby,' Tomas said with a shallow smile. 'If you have not noticed, my sister is a beautiful young woman.'

Kirby nodded. He had noticed, but he didn't feel like discussing his observations with Angela's brother.

Tomas was through talking now. He just stood looking at the hacienda, lost in his own reflections. Again, it wasn't Kirby's place to make a comment, but he did.

'You could go over and mend fences, you know. Get your father's blessing.'

'For what reason!' Tomas reacted angrily.

'It might not mean a lot now, Tomas, but someday it will. This is no way for a son to part from his father. You did it once before, remember?'

'I will consider it,' Tomas said, and Kirby put a hand briefly on Tomas's shoulder before he left him to his thoughts and led the buckskin back to the camp and water.

Before dawn the Mexicans were busy loading the supply wagon with food and necessities. Kirby, riding his big gray once more, saw them load two leather-strapped trunks onto the wagon. So Angela was going. He wondered if she was leaving because it was her father's wish or because it was hers.

He had no time to ponder the girl's motives. The cowboys were gathered at the northern end of the oak grove, grumbling, blowing on cold hands. It was time.

The long drive home was beginning.

They made almost no distance that first day. Just herding the balky longhorns from the canyon, getting them started north with renegade steers bolting in all directions, took all morning and most of the afternoon.

Dallas and the Peck brothers, Tom and Avery, rode the best cutting horses and were the most experienced. They were constantly in motion, riding out to the flanks, hazing the longhorns back into the herd. Dallas on his sorrel, Fargo, was a picture to see, cutting left, right, circling, the sorrel turning on a dime, and seeming to enjoy its work greatly. By nooning horse and man were exhausted, and after coffee and biscuits, Dallas was forced to switch horses as well. He loved Fargo and refused to run the sorrel into the ground for any cause.

They had nooned at a barren patch of open plain where a single mammoth oak tree stood. They could see for miles around. There was nothing but yellow grass. The men ate their meager lunch in silence, growling as they did so before they climbed back into the saddle and rejoined the herd to spell other riders.

The girl stood patiently in the shade of the oak all through the meal. Men glanced at her, but no one spoke or made any remarks. They were too tired for horseplay. Besides, Tomas was constantly nearby.

Angela stood there wearing a white blouse and divided tan riding skirt, high boots and flat-crowned Spanish hat. She was as still and silent as a nun in church. Silent, unmoving. She shared her thoughts with no one else, with the exception of Tomas and even they had little to say to each other. Angela watched the southern horizon. Was she missing her father, the childhood she was now leaving behind her, Kirby wondered.

There was no telling.

He kept his thoughts focused on the job at hand.

The afternoon was kept short intentionally. They came upon a narrow creek a little after four and Colonel Tremaine decided that the men had had enough for the day. Let the cattle drink and bed down. Let the weary men do the same. There was no point in pushing it that first day, perhaps only to end up making dry camp where the surly longhorns would be even more restless and resentful.

'Set up the shifts, Kirby,' Tremaine told him.

'Yes, sir.' A little grimly he added, 'No one's going to be happy about riding night herd tonight.'

'No,' Tremaine said stiffly, 'but they all will take a turn. If anyone complains too much, remind him he's already been paid for this night's work and I expect him to earn his pay.'

'Yes, sir.'

'And, Kirby,' the colonel said, 'if I may make a suggestion . . .'

'Of course.'

'When you arrange the shifts, I wouldn't put Asa and his friends together at any time.'

'Safety first?'

'Exactly. And I'd stick to that all the way back to home range. Keep them separated, especially at night.'

'I'll take your advice.' It was, after all, only common sense. If they were planning to run the herd off; they would have to be together when they made their move.

'I'm thinking three night shifts,' Kirby said. 'Tomas, Bull or myself will be on each one of those watches.'

'Good idea.'

Then the three men the colonel trusted could keep an eye out for any suspicious activities. Though nothing would happen just yet. Asa and his four men could in no way handle the herd, not until they were good and trail-weary. It wouldn't happen for a while.

But both men believed it would happen sooner or later. Assuming the Comancheros left them anything to steal.

The colonel was unsaddling, Kirby sitting the gray

beside him. He looked to the south now, the lowering sun reddening his cheek.

Tremaine asked, 'Escobar? Will he come, Kirby?'

'I don't know, sir.'

'He could be gathering his own forces,' the colonel said, thinking, as always, in military terms.

'Let's hope not. Let's hope the man has enough sense to see it's useless. What is he going to do, kidnap the girl?'

'Maybe he wouldn't have to.'

'What do you mean, sir?'

'What do we really know of all this, Kirby? Perhaps it is only Don Lopez and Tomas who dislike Escobar. A young girl . . . she might find him quite dashing. It could be that she has agreed to this journey only to obey her father, that she would welcome the opportunity to ride off with this dashing *vaquero.*'

This, too, was something to consider. Kirby glanced toward the wagon where they had made a small bed for the girl. The canvas flaps were down, a lantern burned very low behind them.

Maybe so, he considered. Maybe that was why she watched the south constantly, hoping for her lover to rescue her from her father's command. But it was one more thing he couldn't allow himself to dwell on. The herd was his only responsibility at present. Getting it and the colonel safely back to his ranch. For the rest of it – the girl could ride away to China for all he cared.

One thing both he and the colonel had guessed wrong about was figuring that they had a small grace period. That trouble, shooting trouble at least, would hold back for a few days. They were dead wrong about that.

The shooting started that very night.

FIVE

Bull Schultz woke Kirby around midnight. He sat up in his bedroll, looking up at the big man. Bull's broad shoulders blocked out the stars. The night was clear, cold and moonless.

'Second shift already?' Kirby muttered. He had been sleeping soundly but not particularly well, a jumble of meaningless dreams passing through his mind in rapid procession.

' 'Fraid so,' Schultz said.

'Nothing going on?'

'It's quiet as can be. I expected the steers to be a lot more jittery tonight, but I guess that walk was enough to take most of the fire out of 'em.'

'Good,' Kirby said rising, strapping on his gunbelt. 'Where are the boys?' His shift was composed of the Peck brothers, Red and Bobby Stone.

'They're out already. I gave you an extra hour.'

'Thanks,' Kirby said.

'That's all right. But for now, I've had it myself, Kirby.'

The big man ambled off, toting his saddle in one hand, his Winchester in the other. Kirby saddled up in the chill of the night, the gray patiently accepting the cold bit.

Shrugging into his buffalo coat, Kirby glanced toward

the wagon. All quiet there as well. In close proximity to the wagon, Dallas, the colonel and Tomas slept. Each of them, Kirby recalled with a smile, had said the choice of bed site had nothing to do with protecting the girl.

He swung into leather and started toward the herd, shivering while his body slowly warmed inside the heavy coat. He began circling the large bunched steers clockwise, passing Tom Avery within a few minutes.

'Nothing?' he asked Tom, as they paused side by side.

'No, and that's just fine with me,' the lanky, whiskered cowboy answered.

'Me, too.' Kirby started on once more, watching the herd. Only a few were on their feet. Starlight glistened on their horns. Now and then one would gulp or low, but for the most part they were silent, motionless, their legs weary, their bellies full of water.

Perhaps . . .

And then two shots rang out sharply. The longhorns lurched to their feet, startled, but did not run.

Kirby spun the gray around and flicked its flanks with his reins, riding toward the sounds, his rifle unsheathed.

He dipped down into a little gully and started up the far side. At the crest he saw Avery Peck's horse standing, reins trailing, head down.

At its feet lay Avery Peck.

Kirby slowed the gray but did not swing down. Looking from his saddle he could see that Avery was dead. His arms and legs were contorted unnaturally. His eyes were wide open, staring up into the starry sky.

Holding his horse to a walk, Kirby moved on, rifle across the crossbow of the saddle. Behind him he could hear another horse pounding toward him. Tom Peck.

Tom swung down with his horse still on the move and

rushed to his brother, cradling his head on his lap, trying to talk life into his body.

Kirby moved on grimly.

He halted the gray and sat in the night listening and watching. There was a killer out there and he would be wanting to escape. Sooner or later he would have to make a move. Kirby meant to outwait him.

Minutes passed very slowly. There were no audible sounds from the camp. Glancing toward it he saw a lantern lit, no brighter than a firefly from where he sat his horse in the darkness.

Still he waited as the minutes ticked past. Just ahead was a low rise, and Kirby had been looking that way, his eyes fixed on a low star.

And then the star blinked out.

Someone, something had passed in front of the star. Now it blinked on again, and Kirby started that way, the gray moving softly.

He saw the muzzle flash before he heard the bullet whipping past his head. Kirby jammed his heels into the big gray's flanks and went to its side at once. Then he was pounding toward the sniper. A second shot missed wildly as Kirby raced on.

Then up on the rise he saw suddenly the silhouette of a horseman. The sniper's horse reared as he tried to spin away too rapidly, and with a few long strides the gray had Kirby beside the night rider.

Kicking free of the stirrups, Kirby launched himself at the dark figure. His shoulder thudded into the man's ribcage, driving him from the saddle as the horses narrowly avoided a collision, and Kirby and his attacker rolled to the hard earth.

The other man was up first, gun in his hand. Kirby

rolled to one side as the raider's gun spat flame, kicking dirt up into his face.

It was a near shot, but still a miss. Kirby's answering shot, fired from his knees, tagged home.

The gunman buckled at the knees, uttered a strangled moan and pitched forward onto his face.

Kirby rose, trembling, and walked forward cautiously. He kicked the gun away from the man's hand unnecessarily. His bullet had caught the stranger in the heart and he had died instantly. Kirby rolled his adversary over and crouched to look at his face. From behind him now two horses were approaching fast. Kirby spun, gun in hand, but recognized the two incoming riders: Dallas and Len Parker.

Holstering his .44, he stood and took a deep breath of the cold night air, calming himself.

'Are you all right, Kirby?' Dallas asked, dismounting. Len sat his horse, gawking.

'Yeah.'

'Who is it?' Len asked.

'I don't know. Got a match?'

Dallas did and he thumbed it to life. They crouched over the dead man. Kirby had never seen him before. Dallas shook his head. He hadn't either.

'Len?'

'I never seen him,' the cowboy said.

He was a rough-dressed Mexican with a bandido mustache. He carried a knife in his worn boots. His Remington .36 pistol wasn't the best, but it had seen some duty. There was nothing in his pockets except for one ten-dollar gold piece and some smaller Mexican change. No indication of who he had been or where he had come from.

Colonel Tremaine was there now, Bull Schultz with him. Neither of them could identify the raider either.

'Why?' Tremaine asked, puzzled. 'Could he have known Peck, been someone with a long-held grudge?'

'I doubt it, sir,' Schultz said. 'He wasn't long arrived from Kentucky. It would be a hell of a long way to track a man.'

'I don't know him.' This was Tom Peck who had just arrived at the scene of the shooting. 'Besides, my brother didn't have no enemies. He wasn't a troublemaker.'

'Who was he then, and why this?' Tremaine asked.

'I don't think he was after Avery,' Kirby said. 'He was just the first target to present himself. This man – he wanted to kill anybody, anybody at all.'

'But why?' the colonel asked.

'Whittle us down,' Dallas said. 'Just whittle us down little by little. One man at a time.'

Tremaine was startled. It was against his rules of war to act in that way. 'But . . . who?' he asked, truly bewildered.

'Take your choice,' Kirby said. He held out the ten-dollar gold piece. 'I guess this must be the going rate for murdering a cowboy.'

Schultz said, 'We're going to have to change our ways, Kirby.'

'I was already planning on it,' Kirby said. 'I didn't think we'd have to do it until we got further up the trail, but there's no choice now. If they got Avery, they can get any of us.'

'What can we do?' Tremaine asked.

'Outriders, sir. From now on we'll have to free up two men from the herd just to watch the perimeter. Days, they'll ride the flanks, at night circle out wide. It'll mean more work and less sleep for everybody, but it might keep some of us alive longer.'

'Whatever has to be done,' the colonel said. Standing there in the chill of night he looked older, wearier. Perhaps he already regretted his great gamble.

'Daytimes it's me and Dallas on the flanks. Suit you, Dallas?'

'Fine by me,' Dallas answered.

'I doubt we'll have any more trouble tonight, but you might as well roust a couple of extra men. It's not likely anyone will get anymore sleep tonight after word of this gets around anyway.'

'You, Colonel,' Kirby said, 'might as well go back and try to rest, though.'

'Yes,' Tremaine said distractedly, 'yes, I guess I might as well.'

They watched him as he went back to his horse, stiffly swing up and ride back toward the camp. His vigor was already sapped. Kirby was more worried than ever, wondering if the old man was going to survive the long trail home.

'Get on back to the herd, Len. Dallas – no sense in you staying out here.'

'I guess not.' He was still watching Len Parker. 'That look on his face – seems unlikely this was any of Donahue's work.'

'Most unlikely,' Kirby agreed. 'You might as well have Cooky start some coffee and biscuits. We'll be starting early in the morning.'

'All right . . . though I hate to roust him out,' Dallas said. 'You, Kirby? You're not coming into camp?'

'No. My shift isn't finished. Besides, Tom Peck and I have a little work to do. Tom?'

'I'll go get a couple of shovels. Thanks, Kirby.'

Alone again as they rode off, Kirby searched the saddle-bags of the raider's horse. Again there was nothing to be found. The horse carried a Texas brand, Double 'B' connected. That meant nothing. That was an Amarillo ranch, the odds were that the horse had been stolen long ago. Unsaddling the trembling animal, he let it stand while he waited for Tom Peck to come back to bury his brother.

There were no night sounds, no sounds of movement now. Only the occasional lowing of a steer. The night was dead and cold and silent.

As was Avery Peck.

This turn of events bothered Kirby. It was a change in tactics he hadn't considered. He had figured that they would have to stand and fight for the herd somewhere along the long trail home, but it was unnerving to think that the new tactic called for the sniping of individual riders. No pitched battle, no stampeding the herd. Just a slow wearing down. Kirby wondered how many of the colonel's riders would stick now, with this new threat, that of being shot from ambush as they rode night herd or perhaps murdered in their beds by snipers.

How many would just slip away, having no taste for that sort of battle?

Oso. It had to be the Comanchero chief who had planned this. Simply because Donahue wouldn't have made his move this soon. He would want the cattle driven closer to the home range. Escobar? That made no sense. The fiery Mexican might ride in at any time, but he had no particular grudge and no reason to shoot men out of hand. He wanted the girl. Perhaps the herd, although it was of as little use to him as it had been to Don Lopez. Kirby had seen the Escobar land as well. It, too, was poor and dry, over-grazed. It made no sense to name Escobar as the culprit.

No, it was the Comancheros. They were making their move early and in a quite deadly way.

Kirby hardly slept that night. At three in the morning he gave up his shift to Tomas and tried rolling up in his blankets, but it was useless. There was too much to think about.

He had left Tom alone out at his brother's grave. Not out of a lack of compassion, but he knew the Kentuckian would not want to see him crying over that fresh mound of dry earth.

Rising in the morning, Kirby stuffed two biscuits into his mouth and drank some icy water from the barrel on the wagon. That was breakfast. Cooky had sliced and fried some bacon, but Kirby's stomach wasn't up to it that morning. There would be time enough to eat when the drive was done.

With the first light of dawn, they started the longhorn herd across the creek and on toward the broken hills ahead. Sunrise was quick on this cloudless morning. A long golden line across the horizon, a sudden flush of deep pink and then the brilliant sun slowly raising itself. Another clear, cool day would follow, but Kirby was disturbed by the view to the north. There, very low on the horizon he could see clouds massing, dark and flat. The wind was moving toward them, and it was a stiff wind. They would be lucky if they didn't have rain by nightfall.

Kirby and Dallas took the flanks, riding out a quarter of a mile or so from the herd, eyes alert, guns ready. There would be no more sniping if they could help it. Below, Kirby could see the massed herd, moving more easily than yesterday, the chuck wagon well out on the flank to keep the dust out of the food supplies.

The sound of a horse approaching from behind caused Kirby to tense. He turned sharply and then his eyes narrowed with surprise.

It was Angela Trujillo-Lopez, her hat back on its drawstring, black hair drifting in the wind, riding rapidly toward him on the little paint pony Dallas had been using as his second mount.

Kirby reined in and let her catch up with him.

'Hi,' she said breathlessly. She was smiling, her cheeks flushed with the ride. 'Did I surprise you?'

'You could say that, yes,' Kirby answered.

'I couldn't stand the wagon any more. Jolting along in the bed.'

'Did you tell anyone you were leaving?' Kirby asked, as he started his gray forward again, the girl on the pinto beside him.

'The wrangler saddled the horse for me,' she shrugged, 'it was no one else's business.'

'Not Tomas's?'

'No,' she said.

'Or the colonel's? He's responsible for you, you know?'

'I am responsible for myself,' she said saucily. 'Besides, I am with you. Where could I be safer?'

'Right back where you started from,' Kirby said. The girl's carefree attitude annoyed him a little. Sheltered, protected, she seemed to be enjoying her new-found freedom not understanding the risks involved.

'Back in the wagon?' she asked with surprise.

'Right.'

'I didn't like it there. I told you.' She wiped back a strand of raven-black hair from her eyes. 'You are up here.'

'There's a reason I'm up here,' Kirby told her. 'The

same reason you shouldn't be.'

'You mean the man who was shot last night?'

'That's exactly what I mean.'

'They would not shoot me,' she said, with irritating confidence.

Kirby held his tongue. They rode on in silence. He thought Angela would get the hint and ride off, but she didn't seem to mind it a bit.

'I hope it does not rain,' Angela said at length.

Lifting his eyes to the northern horizon, Kirby nodded. The storm clouds he had seen earlier were bunching, lifting their heads high against the pale-blue sky.

'Looks like it will, though,' he said.

'What do you do then? With the cows, I mean?'

'Keep them moving,' Kirby told her, 'and hope for no near lightning.'

For a girl brought up on a cattle ranch she had surprisingly little knowledge of them, it seemed. But, he supposed, she had spent most of her time in the hacienda, knitting or sewing or doing whatever it was cultivated young Spanish women did.

She sure didn't seem to be a bit unhappy about leaving her home, and after a while, Kirby asked her about it.

'It is sad,' Angela said with a small shrug, 'but I have been on the rancho forever! Once a month we would ride to the pueblo to shop, but there is nothing there. Cloth, lace, even buttons and thread have to be ordered from Mexico City, and sometimes from Spain! There was no one to talk to but Father, and he was usually out on the range; I spent most of my time reading.'

'English books, right?'

Angela's dark eyes registered surprise. 'Yes, how could you know that?'

'The way you talk. Never heard a Mexican use English the way you do, like you know it well. Better than me, maybe. Since you've never been away from home, it had to be from books.'

'You are right. Of course I know I make mistakes, but I am proud of the little I do know.'

'You should be,' Kirby said sincerely.

Again, he had no business broaching the subject, but curiosity had been gnawing at him, and so he asked, 'Will you miss Escobar?'

Her eyes became coldly smoldering fire. 'He is a dog! Luis Escobar made it easy for me to decide to journey north.'

'Sorry,' Kirby apologized. 'I just didn't know.' After a moment he said, 'Do you think he'll follow after you?'

'Oh, yes,' she said with conviction. Then her anger returned. 'Luis has had everything he wanted all of his life. One day he decided he wanted me.'

'And your father's rancho?'

'Of course!' Angela said with a half-laugh. 'He wants *everything* and believes it is his right to have it.'

'I see,' Kirby said. That verified some of his conjecture . . . unless Angela was lying to him, and looking at that smooth young face with its high cheekbones, the mouth with the full underlip, which was nearly petulant and quite alluring at once, he decided she was not. Rich girls do not learn to lie well. They seldom need to lie to get what they want.

'And you, Kirby, what will you do if Luis comes?' Angela asked.

'Do?' He fell into thoughtful silence. 'I have no idea. I hadn't thought about it. I suppose if he threatened to take you against your will, I'd have to fight him.'

'Oh?' Her eyes brightened with apparent pleasure.

'The colonel gave your father his word,' Kirby added, and the pleasure in her eyes seemed to fade.

'Then,' she said, 'I hope he does not come. I would not want you to have to fight.'

Kirby didn't understand the girl. This was the first time they had ever spoken, and she acted as if his welfare was of concern to her. But then, Kirby reflected, he really hadn't known that many women with the life he had lived, and the ones he had tried to get to know had confounded him with their thought processes.

He sure didn't know Angela, except for the plain facts. She was pretty, clever, probably more than a little spoiled. What she was made of down deep was a mystery. He shrugged mentally.

'You'd probably better head back now,' he told her. 'The colonel will get worried if he finds you're gone.'

'I suppose so,' she said reluctantly. 'The ride did me good. I am glad we had the chance to talk.' She smiled appealingly. 'Will you ride back with me?'

'I can't. Not until I'm relieved,' he told her.

I see,' Angela answered. Looking over her shoulder, she continued, 'But, look, isn't that your relief rider coming now?'

It wasn't. Kirby looked back as well and saw the man riding toward them at a brisk canter. He sat tall in the saddle atop a black horse with a white tail.

Luis Escobar.

SIX

Escobar was riding alone, but that made him no less menacing. He always sat upright in the saddle, but now his body was stiff with rage, and he slapped his black horse's flank continuously with a silver-handled quirt. As he drew nearer, Kirby could see that his face was set into a mask of fury. Kirby swung down from the gray and waited. Angela stayed mounted, the wind drifting her dark hair prettily. She looked more haughty than frightened. Presumably she had witnessed Escobar's fury before. Kirby had not and he remained ready for anything.

Escobar reined up hard, setting the black nearly on its haunches and leaped from the saddle.

'What are you doing with her!' he screamed at Kirby. Then to Angela: 'Get your things. You are coming home with me.'

'I am not,' she said simply.

Kirby took a moment to scan the countryside behind Escobar. He would not have expected the man to be riding alone.

'I will not have you argue with me. You are betrothed to me.'

'No,' she said, 'I am not.'

Her failure to tremble, to quail, to show any fear at all

seemed to infuriate Escobar further. He stalked to her horse and reached up, grabbing her wrist roughly.

Kirby knocked him down.

He swung a right hand shot from his hip and tagged Escobar on the jaw just below the ear and the Mexican staggered backward, tripped over his own feet and fell to the ground. Sitting there, he rubbed his jaw.

'We don't grab women where I come from,' Kirby said, 'and I don't think gentlemen here do it either.'

'Who are you?' Escobar demanded. His eyes narrowed then, recognizing Kirby from their last encounter. 'You! But your friend is not with you now, is he?'

'Nor are your friends,' Kirby reminded Escobar.

'I should kill you,' Escobar said, struggling to his feet, 'but I think a beating will suffice . . . if you are man enough to fight me when I am looking.'

Escobar was taller than Kirby by three inches, wide in the shoulders, obviously in good shape and proud of it. Kirby sighed heavily.

'I don't want to fight you, no. I just want you to leave the girl alone. Get back on your horse and ride out. It's obvious she doesn't want to go with you, and equally obvious you have no right to force her to go.'

'As I thought,' Escobar smirked, 'a coward.'

'There's no point in it, that's all,' Kirby said. 'I got no personal quarrel with you as long as you leave Angela alone.'

'There is a point to it,' Escobar said, as he unbuckled his gunbelt. 'It would give me great pleasure to beat you. You have struck me, *vaquero*, and I cannot accept such an insult.'

Kirby shook his head slightly. There was no way out of it, it seemed. The man wanted his revenge. Kirby believed that 'honor' had a nothing to do with it. Escobar must have beaten many men in his time, and Kirby guessed he enjoyed the feeling of power it gave him to injure another man.

He bent to untie the thong that held his holster to his thigh and, as he did, Escobar kicked at his head.

Kirby saw it coming and managed to twist aside just a little. The kick, meant to fracture his jaw just grazed his cheek. Before Kirby could get set, Escobar swung his bunched right hand into Kirby's face.

This blow landed flush enough to set the lights flashing in Kirby's head and he staggered backwards. His back came up against the gray horse, which side-stepped away.

As Escobar came in, Kirby jabbed twice with his left, keeping the big Mexican off while his head cleared.

Escobar, already confident of victory, used no science in his attack. He swung wildly with both fists, his eyes alight with dark glee.

Kirby ducked one punch, managed to block another, but a left got through and landed flush against his ear. He felt a trickle of blood begin to flow from it.

Still woozy, but angry now, Kirby also threw caution to the winds and just waded in, firing back with both hands himself.

The two men stood toe to toe, swinging lefts and rights at each other.

Kirby went downstairs, swinging a right into Escobar's stomach. The Mexican grunted and doubled up just a little. Kirby swung a left over the top that landed on Escobar's temple and the bigger man took a step backward. His savage pleasure now became grim determination.

'Stop it!' Angela cried, but she might as well have

shouted to the cold wind, ordering it to stop blowing.

There was no stopping now. Kirby had shaken off the dizziness in his skull and, as Escobar stepped away briefly, Kirby began to move in more methodically. Two jabs and an overhand right followed. The right split Escobar's lip and he muttered a Spanish oath.

Before Escobar could get set again, Kirby shot a second right that caught Escobar on the throat and the Mexican's expression changed again. Now wild concern was in his eyes and he took another half step back as Kirby flailed away. Another left struck home and then he faked with his right. As Escobar flinched away from the anticipated blow, Kirby loaded up a vicious left-hand hook and threw it, catching Escobar flush on the jaw.

The Mexican went to his knees, muttered something incomprehensible and then pitched forward on his face to lie still against the stubble grass.

Kirby stepped away, panting, his fists still clenched tightly. One hand was bleeding. His arms were sore from the pounding they had taken.

He walked to his horse, picking up his hat along the way. The wind gusted over his sweaty body, chilling him. He was breathing raggedly.

Angela just sat her horse staring, not at Escobar, but at Kirby. She was about to speak, but she was interrupted by a distant shout.

Kirby turned, his hand going to his holstered gun, but it was Tomas who was riding toward them at a hard gallop.

'What. . . ?' he shouted as he reined up, but one glance at Escobar told him all he needed to know.

'All your doing!' he shouted at his sister. 'You see what trouble you make? Why are you here?'

'It doesn't matter, Tomas,' Kirby said, swinging wearily

aboard the gray.

'It *does* matter! I am sorry, Kirby, my friend. *You,*' he said, turning again toward his sister, but then he could think of nothing to say. He just shook his head. Escobar was slowly coming to. Tomas dismounted and walked to Escobar's discarded gunbelt, slipping the Colt revolver from the holster. He tucked it behind his own belt and mounted again.

'I came to relieve you, Kirby,' Tomas said in a tight voice. 'Perhaps you would be so good as to escort my sister back to the wagon where she belongs.'

Then he rode to where Escobar's black horse stood and, as Escobar, sitting on the ground, watched, Tomas slapped the black on the rump and sent it trotting away.

'It will take him a little while to catch it up again,' Tomas said. Then to Luis Escobar: 'I think, my friend, you are fortunate that it was Kirby McBride and not me you came to pick a fight with.'

Then Tomas rode away, spurring his horse a little to catch up with the herd.

'Come on,' Kirby said to Angela, and she nodded, following him meekly as he headed down off the rise toward the longhorn herd below. Neither of them so much as glanced back at Escobar.

'I did not mean to cause trouble, Kirby,' she told him.

'It would have happened anyway. One way or the other,' Kirby replied.

'He will not give up this easily,' Angela said.

'I didn't think he would,' Kirby answered.

They passed Bull who was riding drag, and he looked at Kirby's battered face and at Angela riding beside him with curiosity, but he said nothing.

No, Kirby thought, Escobar would not give up. He

would be back, that was certain. Only the next time he wouldn't come alone and he wouldn't be looking for a fist-fight.

When the storm hit it was worse than anyone could have anticipated. Just before sundown the rumbling, anvil-headed thunderclouds darkened the skies, and they could see the harsh flashes of forked lightning above the plains. Thunder rumbled distantly. The longhorns grew progressively nervous as the storm drew nearer and the lightning strikes closer together. The wind increased dramatically. Kirby bowed his head into the wind and rode on. He was riding flank now, trying to keep the long line of steers moving in a straight line. The gray was nervous itself and Kirby couldn't blame the horse. The menacing horns of the steers were too close for comfort, and the lightning continued to strike, the following cannonade of thunder pealing across the land.

Riding up to him, Bull Schultz yelled above the storm, 'We're veering east! Canyon route. It'll give 'em only one way to run – straight ahead, if they decide to stampede.'

Kirby nodded. It was all they could do. He had not seen the long canyon, but Bull had been riding scout earlier in the afternoon and found a route through the broken hills that would help to contain the cattle.

The rain began not with a few isolated drops, but with a sudden torrential rush, falling in an obscuring, pounding screen. Within minutes Kirby could barely see across the herd to the other flank where Tom Peck, clad in a black slicker, his head down, rode.

Within fifteen minutes the ground underfoot was churned to red mud by the passing herd. The wagon was barely making headway. The sun had not yet gone down, but the sky was as black as pitch. Kirby hoped that Tomas, riding point, was steering them correctly toward the canyon route, because he could do nothing but follow along, pinching the herd together.

Lightning struck so near that it startled the gray badly. Kirby could smell sulfur in the air as the following thunder, half a second later, seemed to rock the earth beneath them. The sky went briefly to an incandescent white and then returned to utter darkness, leaving a jumbled image of wet longhorns and riders on Kirby's retinas.

Hours passed with incredible slowness. They seemed to be gaining no ground at all, but Kirby became aware of the land rising beside them, craggy red hills where water streamed in a thousand tangled rivulets. They had made the mouth of the canyon passage at least. Dallas appeared from out of the storm and he leaned near to yell into Kirby's ear above the pitchforks of rain and the eerie howl of the wind. 'Flank riders to the point!'

Kirby nodded his understanding. The walls of the canyon would keep the herd pinched together. Now the thing to do was to gather at the point to try to halt any attempt at a stampede. It was dangerous business, but it would be disastrous to have the steers scatter now. Days could be lost gathering the herd again.

Kirby started toward the head of the herd. He saw Red just ahead of him, his paint pony slogging through the hock-deep mud. Red was bent low in the saddle. Apparently he hadn't gotten the word to move to the point. Kirby approached him and shouted above the whip and roar of the storm.

'Flank riders to the point, Red!'

When Red didn't respond, Kirby reached out and tapped his shoulder.

Red toppled from the saddle to lie face down in the mud as the paint skittered away. Kirby reined up and leaped from the gray's back as the herd lumbered past. Crouching over Red, he turned him face up.

He was dead. There was a bullet hole through his neck. He had been shot by a sniper, and above the wash of the storm, no one had even heard it.

Kirby looked around, scanning the surrounding bluffs, but there was nothing to be seen beyond the curtain of rain. He caught up the shuddering paint pony, hoisted Red across its back and led it forward.

Reaching the point he found the colonel and Asa Donahue in a heated argument. They had reined up at the side of the trail in a shallow hollow at the base of the rising bluff. Kirby rode nearer in time to hear Asa shouting.

'This is crazy! We've got to make camp! We ain't gonna make any more miles today. Not in this!'

'It's better if we keep them moving!' the colonel shouted back.

'The men can't take much more, Colonel! Halt the herd. At least let them have a cup of coffee in shifts!'

'Cooky can't make coffee in this downpour, Asa! Besides, I want these steers as weary as possible before we bed them down! Lessens the risk of a stampede.' The colonel saw Kirby now, and he turned to yell at him. 'What do you think, Kirby—? What happened—?'

Suddenly he was aware of the body thrown over the paint's back and his sentence broke off.

'Is it Red?' Donahue asked.

'Yeah.' Kirby wiped the rain from his face. There was some respite from the storm in the hollow. It was no more than twelve feet deep, but still it was some sort of shelter.

'Who did it?' Asa Donahue demanded. His eyes were fixed angrily on Kirby as if he were responsible.

'A sniper. The same way Avery Peck got it.'

'Why don't they just come down and fight!' Asa said angrily. As much as Kirby disliked the man, he gave him this much – he was genuinely upset about Red's death.

'Why would they come down?' the colonel asked sadly. Then, 'Kirby – keep them going or halt the herd? Donahue says make camp; what do you say?'

Kirby was thoughtful for a moment, then answered, 'Colonel, I'd say keep them moving, except this storm is a lot more than we expected. We can't even see what we're doing out there. I say halt the herd, too.'

Asa appeared surprised that Kirby was agreeing with him. 'Very well,' the colonel said at length. His voice was stiff. He hated to lose any time. He wanted those miles tacked on. So did they all, but conditions were impossible.

'I wanted them too weary to stampede.'

'I know it, sir, but if they were to bolt now, you'd have a crew too tired to control them.'

'All right,' he said, waving a hand in frustration. 'Catch up with point and tell Tomas we're halting. I'll have Cooky set up camp here.' The colonel looked up at the seeping walls of the hollow. 'This isn't much, but maybe he can at least get a fire going in here.'

'I'll see to Red,' Donahue said. His face was drawn and Kirby wasn't sure if it was because Red had been his friend, or simply because Donahue was coming to realize that his men could be shot as well, and if enough of them were killed, it would ruin his scheme to steal the herd.

Kirby rode forward carefully along the herd's flank. A stream was collecting in the bottom of the canyon and mud was beginning to slough off the canyon walls. He

squeezed past the longhorns and finally caught up with
Tomas half a mile ahead.

'The colonel says to hold them up!' Kirby shouted.
Tomas just nodded. He waved Bull over to him and gave
him the word, and the four men on point started to slow
the herd and turn it back on itself.

'Did you see that hollow back a way?' Kirby shouted.
'When you get 'em settled down, tell the boys Cooky
should have some coffee and bacon going in half an hour
or so. You figure out how to divide the shifts.'

Again Tomas just nodded. Shouting above the wind
took more trouble than it was worth unless it was truly
important.

Kirby rode back toward the hollow himself. The cattle
were angry and confused. Bunching up now they bumped
into each other, some going one way, some the other. The
rain made them unhappy and the lightning made them
jittery. There was no graze and no room to lie down. It
would be a rough night trying to keep them calm. Kirby
didn't like to think what a stampede in the close confines
of the canyon on a dark night would be like.

Reaching the hollow again he found the colonel alone,
standing close to a small, smoky fire he had built by throwing together wet wood from the cave, torn branches
deposited there in past floods. The colonel's horse, unsaddled, stood miserably against the back wall.

Kirby swung down and led the gray into the hollow.

'Everything all right up ahead?' the colonel asked.

'Tomas has them turned. It will be all right.'

'For a while?' the colonel said with a thin smile.

'There aren't many guarantees in life, are there, sir?'

'No, no,' the colonel said wearily. 'You're right, of
course, Kirby.'

'We'll make it, Colonel. Nothing worthwhile comes easy.'

'Of course not. I'm sorry, Kirby. A man builds up pictures in his mind of what is to come. Seldom, if ever, are they true to life.' He squatted down and prodded at the poor, smoking fire.

'Where is Cooky?' Kirby asked, looking out into the rain. 'He should have been here by now. Boys will be wanting something hot to eat.'

'It's gotten very muddy out there, Kirby. With the rain and eight hundred steers churning up the ground.'

'Yeah. Maybe I'd better go back and have a look. He might have gotten the wagon bogged down.'

The colonel agreed. 'Yes, maybe you had better. The boys will certainly want a cup of coffee, and I could use a cup myself.'

There was nothing Kirby wanted to do less than to go back out into the teeth of the cold storm, but it had to be done.'

By the time he had tightened his cinches again and started back, the tail end of the herd was just passing, Len Parker and the kid named Archie riding drag. Kirby held Len up and told him what was happening.

'I wondered,' the cowboy growled. 'They were moving almighty slow.'

'Where's Cooky?' Kirby asked.

'You know that's funny,' Len said, looking back. 'He was right behind us, but in this rain. . . .' He shrugged. 'Can't be too far back.'

Kirby started on. The rain and wind were at his back now, but that was little relief. It was still cold and his buffalo coat was heavy with rain over his damp shoulders. He did have a slicker in his roll, but there hadn't been time to dig it out before the storm hit; besides a slicker offered little warmth.

He slogged on, the gray hock-deep in cold mud now. The cattle had churned up the ground horribly. The odds were good that Cooky had gotten stuck. Hopefully he hadn't broken a wheel or an axle! That would delay them interminably.

A quarter of a mile on he still found nothing. He was alone in the cold night. Pausing, he listened, hoping to hear the creak of wagon wheels and harness, but the night was still except for the wind.

For a time there was a silver ghost of a moon beaming through the sheer clouds, and it was by this meager light that Kirby stumbled across some sign: the ruts cut by wagon wheels into the mud; overlaying the tracks of the cattle, they were clearly visible. Then the sky closed up again, the moonlight fading, and Kirby swallowed a curse.

The tracks he had found were not heading northward, following the herd, but had veered off sharply toward the east and the shallow draw he had seen.

Why? Cooky couldn't have mistaken the trail, and he wouldn't have pulled aside even if he were breaking down. There could be only one explanation.

Someone had taken the wagon and captured Angela as well!

SEVEN

Kirby rode with supreme caution. The night was foul and dark, the wind whistling down the canyon eerily. The rain came in sheets, cleared briefly and then would wash down again in a hammering assault.

He had guided the big gray horse into the wash, but now he more or less let it have its head. He could not see clearly enough to guide it further.

Now and then the gray misstepped, jolting Kirby's spine. The ground underfoot was treacherous. There were many round rocks along the trail – if trail it could be called – the earth cleared from the stones by the rain.

He strained his eyes against the coal-black darkness, looking for a silhouetted image, a flash of white which might be the canvas top of the supply wagon, but for minute after interminable minute, he saw nothing.

He estimated he had been riding in that lonesome draw for half an hour at least when his search was rewarded.

The wagon stood in the road ahead of him, silent and unmoving. The horses had been unhitched. Eyes narrowing, Kirby continued on, very slowly now, approaching the wagon up a slight grade. The walls of the canyon rose around him, and the air had gone suddenly still and colder yet.

Nothing moved.

He dismounted twenty yards from the wagon and approached it with ultimate care, Winchester in his hands. His boots slipped on the mud as he crept toward the wagon. Everywhere else in the night was as still and silent as a tomb.

Reaching carefully for the flap of the canvas, he took a deep breath and threw it back, pulling away, rifle to his shoulder, but there was no response.

It was empty except for Angela's bed.

The supplies had all been taken. Horseshoes, ammunition, sugar, bacon, beans, flour. Everything usable. Everything they desperately needed for the drive. The men, he thought drily, would be eating a lot of beef from here on.

He circled the wagon slowly as a light rain fell again. There was no sign of anyone. Blessedly, no corpses on the ground.

So, then, what had become of Angela and the cook? Could they have gotten stuck and decided to cut the horses free of their traces and ridden on? No. The wagon was not bogged down on that stony trail, and that theory would not explain the missing supplies.

They had been ambushed, that was certain.

Kirby stood, one hand on his hip, the other dangling the rifle, looking ahead – for it was certain they had been taken that way. He had passed no one coming up the trail, and the high walls enclosing the draw allowed no passage either right or left. Searching the ground for tracks was fruitless, as he had expected. Any sign would have been washed away almost immediately by the falling rain.

There was no choice. Kirby mounted again and started the gray forward toward the distant head of the draw, not knowing where it led or who waited there.

He soon discovered why whoever had captured the wagon had chosen to abandon it. The road narrowed rapidly and began to climb more steeply, the canyon walls closing in so there was barely room for two horses to pass side by side. Water rushed past beside the trail, a narrow, fast-moving creek racing toward the canyon floor below. Visibility was nil.

Kirby saw the gunman rise from the dark ground and he fired at the silhouette he presented, but he was a fraction of a second too slow. The sniper's gun fired in return and a sudden jarring pain flooded Kirby's skull and he fell awkwardly from the rearing gray's back, landing hard. He saw the gray start away at a trot and tried to get to his feet to prepare himself for a fight, but the Winchester had slipped from his numb fingers and there was blood in his eyes. There was a momentary flash of color in his skull, like close-exploding fireworks, and then everything went cold and utterly black.

The silver rain was falling into his eyes. He was too stiff to attempt movement. Kirby tried lifting his head, but that simple effort sent a bolt of pain through his entire body. He lay back, closing his eyes again. He was very cold, but he was alive. Maybe. In those first few waking minutes he wasn't even sure of that; then logic told him no one could feel so cold and wet and be dead.

He moved his hand, searching for his Colt. If he at least had that . . . he did, but curiously, he discovered with his moving fingertips that someone had thrown a blanket over him. He opened his eyes and looked down painfully. True. Someone had thrown a red and white Indian blanket over him. His fogged mind struggled with that concept. Someone had ambushed him and then come to cover him with a blanket?

'You're awake! Don't move, Kirby. I couldn't get you anywhere drier. And there isn't anyplace, anyway.'

It couldn't be, but it was. Kirby saw Angela walk to him, her face drawn with concern. She knelt down beside him.

'I tried to bandage your head. I'm afraid I didn't do a very good job. But the wound isn't as bad as it probably feels.'

'Where in hell . . . what happened, Angela?' Kirby demanded. He tried to sit up, failed, and settled for leaning back on his elbows as the concerned girl hovered over him, her lips pursed with concentration as she examined his head.

'The man who shot me . . .'

'You got him too,' Angela said. 'I found his body. I never saw him before.'

'Where's Cooky? What happened?'

'Just a minute and I'll tell you. You've got to sit up. Can we get you against that boulder? Try it. I'll help you.'

That accomplished, Kirby sat there dizzily, his back propped against a cold reddish boulder the size of a wagon. Angela examined his head wound again, clicked her tongue, and bound it up once more.

'You need some stitches. Your scalp has been laid open.'

'Tell me,' Kirby said, spacing his words out carefully, 'what happened to you.'

Angela wiped back her hair and settled beside him with a sigh.

'The rain got really heavy, as you know, and we started falling further and further behind. Cooky was cussing fiercely at the team, but they couldn't do any more than they were already doing. Once we got bogged down to the axle, but somehow we got out of the mud.

'I wasn't contributing anything, and Cooky growled at me to just lie down in the back and go to sleep if I could. It was so cold that I crawled under the blankets just to keep warm although I knew I wasn't going to sleep.

'Then I heard someone shout – in English – I didn't get the words, but Cooky halted the team. I thought it was you, or someone from the crew, but when I looked up. I could see that Cooky was holding his hands in the air, and a man climbed up on the seat beside him with a drawn gun.

'He ordered Cooky to turn the wagon and start up this draw. There were three men altogether – or that's how many I heard anyway. I stayed under the blankets, petrified that they might find me.

'It was slow-going up the trail. It's pretty steep and slick as you know, and the team was struggling mightily. Finally we stopped and I heard the men talking loudly. They decided to cut the team loose and use them for pack animals. That meant they were going to unload the wagon. My heart started pounding crazily. I knew they'd find me in the wagon, so I eased back toward the tailgate. It was very dark, the rain pounding down. I didn't see anyone, so I figured they couldn't see me. I slipped out of the wagon and hid in a stack of boulders beside the road.

'I watched them unload the wagon in the dark and load the provisions onto the horses. I waited a long time yet, not moving. When they were gone, I went back to the wagon and snatched the blankets from it. They had left them, thank goodness. Then I found better shelter and hid there to wait until daylight.'

'What happened to Cooky?' Kirby asked.

'I don't know,' she said worriedly. 'I thought I heard a shot once, but I might have been mistaken. The storm was clattering over, making so many noises. I think they just took him along with them.

'Then you came along,' Angela continued. 'I was up ahead about fifty yards or so, and I started back toward you, blankets over my head, wading through the mud. I saw the man with the rifle leap up from behind the rocks, saw him shoot . . . it almost stopped my heart. When you fired back, he went down and stayed there.

'I came to you, but there was nothing I could do but cover you up and wait, hoping none of the other raiders came back to see what had happened to their friend.'

'My horse. . . ?'

'He's OK. He didn't want to wander far from you, I guess. I found him and took him back to where I had been hiding.'

'That's something to be thankful for,' Kirby said. His head was throbbing miserably and he was sick to his stomach with the pain.

'What do we do now?' Angela asked. Her eyes were anxious. She was badly frightened.

Kirby looked to the morning skies. Still the rain fell, but not nearly so hard as in the night past, and there was enough gray light to see by. 'We head back to the herd. There's nothing else to do.'

'What about Cooky?'

Kirby shook his head. 'We don't know where they went. We can't track them under these conditions. If we did find them, what could we do against a band of armed men? I'm sorry for Cooky, but for now he's on his own.'

'I understand,' Angela sighed. 'I wish we could help him, but I can see it's impossible.' She asked, 'Kirby? You

85

. . . can you ride?'

'There's not much choice,' he said grimly. 'I can ride out of here or sit in the rain waiting to see if those gunmen do come back. I'll ride.'

It would be slow going with the two of them on the gray, but with luck they should be able to catch up with the herd by midday.

Kirby was studying Angela's intent face. He had wondered what the girl was made of down deep, thinking she was probably just being foolish in her bravery before Escobar. Now his opinion was beginning to change. There was no crying, no hysterics. She had done what she had to do as well as she could and had done it quite bravely. She would do.

Angela went to retrieve the gray, vanishing into the rain and, while she was gone, Kirby dragged himself to his feet. Such a simple little thing it was, getting to your feet. But not just then. He turned, braced himself against the rock and got to his knees. Pain tore through his body and he had to stay there, unmoving, for half a minute. Gradually he levered himself upright. He stood, back against the damp boulder, his head swimming crazily. At least he was up. Staying in the saddle for many miles would prove much more difficult.

He tried to analyze their situation, but his thoughts refused to organize themselves. It was the Comancheros who had raided the wagon, of course. More of their guerilla tactics of pecking away at the herd, depriving them now of their needed supplies and, incidentally, capturing a prize.

Had it been Escobar, he would have known that Angela was in the wagon. Besides, Angela had said the men spoke in English. Although Escobar did know the language, it was not his native tongue and it was unlikely all of his men spoke it or that he would lapse into it at a time like this.

Comancheros.

Colonel Tremaine would be wondering what had happened to the wagon, and to Kirby and Angela. They had to reach him as soon as possible. Kirby looked longingly at the wagon. He could have used a nap in the back of it for a few hours himself.

'Kirby!' Angela's voice was not loud, but worried. In the rain she had lost her position.

'Right here,' he said, and she came forward, leading the gray which seemed happy to see its master upright, alive. Kirby stroked the animal's muzzle and looked to the saddle that had never seemed so high before.

'I'll need some help, I'm afraid,' he said, a little embarrassed to admit it.

'Let's get you up one way or the other,' Angela said. 'We've got to get going.'

'Right. First,' Kirby directed, 'get into my bedroll and take out the slicker. 'You're already pretty soaked, but it might be some help.'

That done, Angela dressed in his black slicker, the sleeves rolled back, helped Kirby into the saddle. He sat there precariously, head reeling. Angela got up easily behind him and they started down the trail toward the canyon floor.

The rain had slowed, but the water that had fallen ran swiftly down the canyon bottom now, forming a fast-moving creek quite shallow, but twenty feet wide. They had to hug the bluffs, and there the mud was very thick as the sodden earth sloughed off.

It was a chill and uncomfortable ride. The only small comfort for Kirby was the touch of the slender arms wrapped around his waist.

Around noon, Angela asked, 'Where can they be? I thought you told me we should be able to see them by now.'

'I thought so. Maybe the colonel decided to drive them on through the night after all.'

The canyon pass began to peter out, the land flattening around them, and they found themselves on the plains once again. Low broken hills no more than a few hundred feet high crowded the horizon beneath shifting silver-black skies.

'Which way have they gone?' Angela asked, as they sat the gray, resting for a moment.

'I don't know.' Even the big herd would have left no sign of its passing through that heavy rain. 'All we can do is strike out north toward the home ranch. We'll find them somewhere along the way.'

'If only the skies would clear,' she said, and he felt her shiver.

If only so, but in the early afternoon it got worse, much worse, with the thunderstorms beginning again, bone-white lightning streaking hotly across the sky, illuminating their landmark red mesa only intermittently. By the flashes they saw nothing moving on the plains, and when the lightning flickered out they saw nothing at all. They picked their way over the broken land.

Kirby felt it coming, but he could not stop it. Exhausted, still stunned, he felt his grip on the reins fail him and then his spine seemed to be torn from his body so that he went as limp as a wash rag.

'Angela . . .' he said, and then he fell from the horse and landed in an unconscious heap against the cold, red ground.

When Kirby's eyes opened it was to total confusion. He was on his back, and above him was a patch of sky where now and then a star blinked on. The air was still around him, a strange sensation in itself after the days of harsh winds. He was in some sort of shelter, but what kind? Where?

'Back with us, are you?' The voice from the darkness was Angela's. Lifting his head slightly, he could see her eyes by the feeble starlight.

'Where. . . ?' he began, and tried to sit up.

'It's all right. Take it easy.'

'Where in blazes are we, Angela! And how did I get here?'

Kirby managed to sit up. It didn't hurt half as much as it had that morning, but a gang of little men with tiny sledgehammers still seemed to be at work behind his eyes.

'You passed out. I put you over the horse's back and kept on, toward the northern mesa.'

'You put me on my horse!' Kirby said in astonishment. Angela could not have weighed much more than 100 pounds, and Kirby was a lean but solid 170.

'Pretty strong, huh?' she asked with a smile. She pretended to make a muscle with her right arm. 'I didn't say it was easy,' she added.

'It stopped raining for awhile, and I saw this little notch on the mesa face. I headed up to it, and that's where we are. It's not much but it beats being in the weather. I had a fire for a while, but I kicked it out after dark.'

'Good girl,' Kirby said approvingly. Half the women he knew wouldn't have been able to start a fire in these damp conditions, let alone have the sense to put it out after darkness fell. He was sitting up now. He saw the bulky silhouette of his gray horse in the back of the notch, unsaddled, munching on some tufts of bunch grass she had pulled up for it. Overhead there was a wedge of sky. Across the gap a huge old pine tree had fallen and it offered some protection from any rain that might fall. Not much – but it was something. All in all, the girl had done good.

'Any water?' Kirby asked

'Your canteen's beside you. And there were a few biscuits in your saddle-bags. What do you do, squirrel those things away?'

'I always grab a few extra. Can't ride in from the range every time I get a little hungry. Old habit.'

'I'm glad you have it,' Angela said sincerely. 'I ate a few of them myself.'

'And welcome to them,' Kirby said. Then, after drinking from the canteen and munching on a dry salt biscuit, he said, 'We sure haven't done much of a job of protecting you, have we?'

'There wasn't much anyone could have done,' she said casually. 'Think, Kirby, if you'd been there when the raiders came, they would have shot you down.'

'I guess so.'

Now he got to his feet again. After the expected dizziness passed, he found he didn't feel half bad. He walked to the mouth of the notch which was thirty or forty feet deep by twenty feet high. The floor was level, a few fallen boulders scattered about. One wall of the notch was smoked. Earlier travelers or Indians had used this for shelter before.

He stood in the mouth of the notch, looking out across the land. They were fifty feet or so above the flats. A rugged trail could be seen descending. Beyond, the land was still and dark. A jumble of rugged hills and two jutting mesas, backlighted now by the soft glow of a coming moon still below the horizon, but promising to rise early.

He said with a smile in his voice, 'Well, we don't seem to be gaining ground real fast, do we?'

'No,' she answered. Angela was sitting on the ground, her knees drawn up, arms looped around them, hair down, gathered loosely at the nape of her neck with a ribbon. The glow of the rising moon caught her face prettily.

'I went out earlier and listened,' Angela said. 'I couldn't hear a thing. Only stillness. I thought maybe I heard cattle lowing once, but I'm afraid it was imagination. We must be miles from the herd.'

'Yes, we must,' Kirby agreed. Although in what direction he had no idea. Tomas might have guided them further east or west for reasons not apparent.

Angela was beside him now and he was surprised to feel her hand rest gently on his shoulder. 'Everything could be worse,' she said. 'They could have captured me. They could have shot you dead.'

'Which is probably what everyone believes did happen to us,' Kirby reflected.

'Will they send someone back to look for us?'

'How can they? They can't spare any men. Even having one man gone would be a big loss, and no man would be sent back alone into this situation. No, we'll have to make our own way out.'

Kirby started to continue, 'When they discover—' Then he fell silent abruptly and put his arm around Angela's shoulder, whispering harshly, 'Get down!'

'What. . . ?' But then she, too, saw the line of riders on the flats below them.

Kirby counted six men approaching from the south in

a ragged line, moving directly toward the notch where he and Angela were hiding.

'Get my rifle!' he said sharply into her ear, and she backed away to where Kirby's gear lay, scuttling back in a half-crouch, Winchester in hand. They lay flat, watching the dark riders approach. Glancing toward the back of the notch, Kirby saw the gray's head come up alertly. Ears pricked. He prayed the animal wouldn't whicker.

The arc of the rising moon was visible now, full and deep orange. Fantastic night shadows crept out from the feet of the landforms and the few broken trees and jumbled cactus beyond.

Angela gasped and clutched Kirby's forearm. She placed her lips beside his ear. 'It's Luis!'

Kirby nodded. He had already been able to distinguish the silver-mounted saddle on the lead horse, and now, by the glow of the ascending moon, he could make out the figure on its back that could only be Luis Escobar.

Oddly, that caused Kirby to relax just a little. Escobar could not know of the notch's existence . . . or could he? Perhaps one of his riders was familiar with this country. There was no point in speculating. They could only lie still and watch and wait, Kirby's hand clamped around the Winchester's trigger as the hunters drew nearer.

EIGHT

The riders on the flat below halted on the trail and there was conversation, none of which Kirby could understand across the distance. One of the riders lifted a hand and seemed to point directly at them, but Escobar said something roughly, and they started on again, moving northward across the moon-glazed plains.

Kirby watched them until the last horseman was out of sight, then, taking a deep breath, he sat up beside Angela. Her shoulder was next to his and he could feel her trembling.

'He terrifies me,' she said.

'I wouldn't have known, the other day.'

'That—' she said disparagingly, 'that was for his benefit. I will never let him know how much I fear him. There is something evil in his heart, Kirby.'

'Yeah, I know.' Because Kirby felt it too. There was something, if not evil, bordering on the abnormal about Escobar. His arrogance, his belief that only he was right, that he deserved everything he wanted, that no one could thwart him, indicated a twisted mentality. If he had ever married Angela, what then? Would he have hurt her, abused her? Kirby didn't allow himself to dwell on those dark thoughts.

'Now what can we do?' Angela asked, her voice suddenly very small.

'Nothing much. Rest up a little and then ride – carefully – after the herd.'

'You can sleep!' she asked in astonishment.

'Not me,' Kirby said with a smile. '*You*, girl. I'm going to sit up and keep watch. I don't think they'll be back, but you can never be sure. Besides,' he said, 'I've had my rest.'

'I can't sleep.'

'You can try. You'll need it.'

'I suppose so,' she said, and then reluctantly she stood, rubbing her arms against the cold. She walked to where the blankets lay and tried her best to roll up in them comfortably. Despite her protests, she was asleep within minutes. Her easy breathing was a comforting sound in the night. He shifted position, sitting cross-legged, back against the wall of the notch, watching the flats below until the full moon had begun to fade and the long hours passed into early dawn.

With the sky in the east gray and colorless, they started on. Kirby followed Escobar's tracks far enough to assure himself of the Mexican's direction, then angled slightly eastward, still heading generally north, but away from Escobar's route.

The question was – was he also veering away from the route the herd had taken?

He tried to keep to the high ground when possible, and now and then would swing down to search the far horizons for sign of the herd, for smoke, color, anything – but nothing seemed alive on all the broad plains.

'Are we in Texas yet?' Angela asked, as the morning wore on.

'Not until we cross the Rio Grande,' Kirby answered.

'And I can't see it ahead anywhere either. If I didn't know better, I'd swear we were riding in circles.' They seemed to be gaining no ground whatsoever. The endless slow plodding miles passed, the land changing only little from hour to hour

The storm had broken, the sky cluttered with huge billowy white clouds, and the wind had returned to chase them. The ground underfoot was drying rapidly as the thirsty earth soaked up the rain. They began to find grass now, and from time to time they let the weary gray graze while they sat resting. Losing more ground, Kirby reflected, but the patient horse had to be given whatever food, water and rest they could allow it.

Just before sundown, weary and saddle-sore, Kirby saw the long silver ribbon in the distance, and he halted the horse.

'There it is,' he said, pointing, 'the Rio Grande. Texas across the river.'

'And the herd?'

Still they had not seen the herd. Kirby began to feel vaguely guilty. He should be with the colonel, helping him, watching his back. Had Donahue made his move? Had the Comancheros struck?

They made a dry camp on a low knoll where a dozen live oaks grew. They had seen a few deer, many rabbits, but Kirby hadn't dared shoot anything, and so their stomachs contracted and growled as they ate the last few biscuits and drank the canteen empty.

'You never thought the trip to your aunt's home would be like this, did you?' Kirby asked, as they sat together, watching the sunset spread grandly over the western hills. The land flushed to a deep red and the sky went briefly to gold and vermillion.

'No,' Angela said, looking up at him with those huge brown eyes. 'I didn't think it would be like this.'

She meant something more, Kirby decided, but he did not know women that well, and he wasn't sure what it was exactly that she intended. He didn't dare hope ... he didn't dare hope, and that was that.

They rolled up in their blankets, the horse pegged out between them, and slept early. Wearily, Kirby closed his eyes. He felt much better than the day before, although his scalp was itching terribly and he couldn't scratch it. He still had a dull headache and his shoulder hurt from the fall from the gray, but it was manageable pain. He had hurt worse in his life. He slept.

Sometime after midnight he came awake instantly, although he did not move from his bed.

Someone was out there. The moon had not yet risen and all he could see were the dark forms of the oaks, their upper branches moving gently in the night breeze. Glancing at the gray, he could see its head up, its ears pricked.

What, then?

Even in his sleep he had heard something. Some small sound that had awakened him instantly. As his hand slid to his holstered Colt and drew it, he heard it again.

A tiny sound, a foot passing softly over twigs and leaves.

And then he saw the man with the drawn gun appear at the fringe of the shadows and Kirby rolled from his bed, going to one knee, cocked Colt steady in his hand.

'Hold it right there. You're in my sights!'

'And you're in mine,' the familiar voice drawled, 'but I ain't going to shoot you, Kirby.'

'Dallas!'

'None other. I thought it was you, but I couldn't tell for

sure,' the blond cowboy said, holstering his gun.

'Why,' Kirby asked, 'aren't you with the herd?'

'What herd?' Dallas said, sagging to the ground. He was hatless, and Kirby noticed his shirt was torn at the shoulder and the knee was out of his jeans.

Dallas noticed Angela for the first time as she rose from her bed and he said, 'Well, at least you're OK – that's something to be thankful for.'

'What happened, Dallas?' Kirby asked worriedly.

'They hit the herd. It happened not long after you left. Half the boys had gone back for coffee and grub, expecting Cooky to show up. Me, Tomas and Tom Peck were trying to hold the herd in a bunch.

'They came out of the rain before we saw them, let alone had a chance to fight back. They shot old Fargo out from under me and I rolled to the ground hard. I guess I was out for a minute or two. I couldn't see a thing in the confusion. Riders, cattle, lightning and fury. I hotfooted it toward a low knoll. I saw someone down on the ground. I don't know who it was. I couldn't stop to check.'

'Tomas!' Angela exclaimed, her fingers to her lips.

'I just couldn't see. Everything was moving shadows and gunfire.'

'Comancheros?' Kirby asked.

'Of course. There were maybe twenty of them. I laid low for a few hours. The herd was moved out. There was nothing I could do to stop it. Not on foot, especially.'

'The colonel. . . ?'

'I'm coming to that,' Dallas said. 'I walked all the way back to the hollow. Len was there. And the kid, Archie. Both dead. The colonel was gone.'

'Then he may be alive.'

'May be,' Dallas shrugged, 'may be not. I didn't want to

stay there, not knowing if they might come back, so I started toward where I thought you were with the wagon. I couldn't find you either! Rain was so heavy and it was as dark as stink.'

'Yeah, we know.'

'But I had one stroke of luck. A straggler, I guess, a rear guard maybe. Anyway, one of the Comancheros came riding up the canyon on that bay horse I've got now.'

'What happened?' Angela asked.

'I told you,' Dallas said deliberately. 'I got the bay horse now.'

'How'd you find us?' Kirby wondered.

'Pure chance. By the way, did you know Luis Escobar's riding around out there still?'

'We know. We saw them.'

'Crazy fool. He's lucky if he doesn't ride straight into the Comancheros himself.'

Kirby was silent, thinking, trying to formulate some sort of plan. Finally he said, 'There's nothing you can do, Dallas. Maybe you ought to chuck it and ride back to Texas.'

'Fat chance!' the cowboy said indignantly. 'I ride for the brand. Besides,' he said with a lowered voice, as he glanced at Angela, 'I came down here hunting Comancheros, remember? Now I found me some. And with that herd, come daylight, I'll find them.'

'*We'll* find them,' Kirby amended. 'I don't know what we can do, but if there's a chance the colonel, Bull Schultz, Tomas are still alive, we'll find them. If only we could catch up another horse . . .'

'For what?' Angela asked with suspicion.

'For you, of course. We could get you across the river and started toward your aunt's house in San Antonio.

Then Dallas and—'

'No!' Angela interrupted. 'What is it that Dallas said – "Fat chance"? Well, fat chance with me too, Kirby.'

'You are not going to go chasing a band of bloodthirsty Comancheros with us,' Kirby said firmly.

'And who will stop me? Besides, who is to say they will not find me out there by myself?'

'The lady has a point,' Dallas commented.

Kirby supposed she did, but how were they supposed to get anything done with Angela tagging along? It was a reckless enough plan as it was, one only undertaken because he had committed himself to the job, to the colonel. He stood looking at her face, the set jaw and determined eyes.

'They may have my brother,' she reminded him.

'You won't be any help to us.'

'Have I been of no help to you the past few days?' Angela shot back hotly.

'This is different.'

'Nothing is different. I, too, have a sense of duty, Kirby. If not to a herd of cows, to my family at least. To Tomas.'

That seemed to settle things. Kirby could think of no rebuttal. Besides, they did not have a third horse. There were only two choices – ride away himself, taking Angela with him, or lead her into a fight with the Comancheros.

Finally he said with disgust, 'All right, then. Come with us.'

'I've got a spare rifle she can have,' Dallas said. 'It came with the horse.'

'I can shoot,' Angela said eagerly. Kirby said nothing in reply. He walked away from the two of them to stand brooding, staring out over the plains from the mouth of the notch. He stood there a silent minute before he felt

Angela's hand slip under his arm and he turned to face her.

'It will be all right, Kirby. I will not get in your way.'

Her small bravery touched him. What would he do if something happened to her? These last few days his feeling toward Angela had changed dramatically. Too dramatically. He couldn't stand the thought of anything hurting her – ever again.

They walked back to where Dallas, after leading the bay horse up the knoll, had promptly rolled up and gone to sleep. Neither Angela nor Kirby felt like sleeping any more, and they spent the remainder of the night in silence, sitting side by side, watching the stars blaze away in a cobalt sky, seldom speaking, not feeling the need for speech.

With the morning sun, Dallas rose from his bed. He sat there for a minute, blankets wrapped around his shoulders, rubbing his head. Kirby had saddled the gray already. Angela, appearing tense but determined, watched him slip the bit into the horse's mouth.

'I'm the late one, huh?' Dallas said around a yawn.

'No hurry.'

'I guess not.' He got to his knees and rolled his blankets. Over his shoulder, Dallas said, 'How about some chow?'

'We don't have anything,' Angela answered.

Dallas rose, grinning, his blanket roll over his shoulder. 'I should have told you – look in the saddle-bags off the bay. The Comanchero rider was carrying some food. It's not much, some tinned tomatoes and some salt pork. Now, that isn't much of a meal . . . unless you two are as hungry as I am.'

They ate the odd breakfast with restrained relish. No, it wasn't much, but it would keep them going for one more day. After that, Kirby reflected, there might not be any further need for food.

'You figured where they're headed?' Kirby asked Dallas.

'East. I tracked them until I lost the moon last night. The ground is still wet. They're leaving deep tracks.'

'East?' Kirby glanced that way, toward the red mesas and tangled hills. 'I wonder why.'

'My guess is that's where they have their hideout. They never meant to sell those steers. They mean to keep 'em for a food supply.'

'Or hold them until they can rebrand them,' Kirby suggested.

'Maybe you're right there,' Dallas said, 'but they're heading east, all right. We should be able to pick up their trail easy enough. We'll catch up with 'em, and soon. Which suits me fine,' he added.

'Caution, Dallas,' Kirby said, raising his eyes in Angela's direction. 'We must remember to use some caution.'

'I know, Kirby,' Dallas said, as he hefted the bay's saddle, 'it's just that I've been waiting a long time to get in my licks against the Comancheros. I saw their leader yesterday. Funny, not long ago some of the boys were talking about him.'

'About who?' Angela asked.

'Why, the one-armed man. That renegade marshal from Lawrence, Kansas.'

Tal. Kirby felt his blood go cold. His eyes were fixed oddly on Dallas. It couldn't be! Dallas was saying that Tal McBride, Kirby's own brother, was the Comanchero leader, Oso. Impossible! The West was full of one-armed men after the war. There had to be a mistake. But Tal *had* been the town marshal in Lawrence for a while. Kirby had tracked him that far.

'What was his name?' Kirby asked tightly. Dallas glanced at him and shrugged, tightening his cinches.

'I can't recall. I just remember Donahue, Red and some of the other boys talking about this one-armed marshal in Lawrence. They had a run-in with him once, it seems.'

'How do you know it was him you saw last night?' Kirby asked too sharply so that Dallas was put on his guard.

'Why, I don't know for sure, I guess, Kirby. But the way the boys were talking . . .'

'They were wrong,' Kirby said. His eyes were like flint. Dallas glanced at Angela and shrugged it off.

'If you say so, Kirby.'

'I say so.'

'Sure. All right,' Dallas said. Then with a second glance at Angela who was obviously as puzzled as he was, Dallas went to saddle the bay horse.

'What is it, Kirby?' Angela asked, coming nearer, looking at his set features. 'What's wrong?'

'Nothing is wrong,' Kirby said, and he turned his back on her and walked to the gray, swinging up into the saddle.

He sat silently, the wind playing through the horse's mane, waiting as a perplexed Angela gathered her few things and, after a word to Dallas which elicited only a shrug, walked to him.

Kirby was confused and upset. He *knew* Dallas was wrong about Tal. The blond cowboy had simply heard two different camp-fire stories and put them together since each involved a one-armed man.

That was all there was to that. Wasn't it?

Kirby was sure of one thing: he now had another powerful reason to find the Comancheros, and that he would do. He had to know one way or the other. He looked grimly at Angela as she approached with her bedroll. He wished to blazes there was something to be done with her, some way to send her away and to protect her from what was to come, but there was no hope of that. There was no sheltering church, no nearby towns.

'I said it will be all right, Kirby,' she said, resting one hand on his leg as she looked up at him with those wide brown eyes.

'Will it?'

She did not understand the tone of his voice, this different side of Kirby McBride. What was it that was troubling him? She swung up behind him, his strong assisting grip on her wrist.

One part of the problem was solved early on that morning. In an arroyo where water trickled thinly, they found an abandoned horse, its saddle upside down. They caught up the mournful-looking animal without much trouble. It wasn't until they had saddled it properly and gotten Angela aboard the little blue roan that Dallas said quietly to Kirby, 'That was Tomas's second mount.'

Kirby glanced at horse and rider. Angela was unaware of the fact that the roan had been Tomas's spare, taken out of the colonel's string.

'No point in mentioning it to her,' Kirby said.

'I wouldn't think of it,' Dallas answered.

Then they started east again, riding directly into the rising sun. Kirby decided that the three of them were all crazy. Riding after twenty Comancheros. Hoping to accomplish what, exactly? Capture the criminals? Free the colonel and his hands? There was a good chance they had all been killed anyway. Of what use would they be to Oso after he had used them to drive the steers home? Why hold and feed useless hostages?

Kirby's thoughts were running along these paths when Dallas, riding ahead of him, lifted his hand, halting his bay horse.

'It looks like we found 'em,' Dallas said, as Kirby reached his side, and Kirby nodded.

The passing herd had left a wide swath of tracks a blind man could follow in a fog and, true to Dallas's reckoning, they were heading eastward, into the dry tangled hills ahead. 'They'll have guards out. Outriders,' Dallas said, as they continued on. 'Once we get into the hills, we're sure to be spotted.'

'Do you know the area, Dallas?'

'Not at all,' the cowboy answered.

The Comancheros had all the advantages. They had the high ground, they had the numbers, they knew the area.

'You could still track off,' Dallas reminded Kirby. 'Take the girl and head for the Rio Grande.'

'And you?'

'Me?' Dallas shrugged. 'I'm going on, Kirby, you know that.'

'Some lone angel of retribution?'

'Something like that. You can't know what it's like to come home . . . to what used to be home and find all you loved in the world destroyed. Dead.'

Dallas spoke softly, but the emotion was electric in his eyes.

'If only I could convince Angela to ride for the river,' Kirby mused.

'Well, if I know her, you can't. Besides, Kirby, it's like she said before – a woman out here alone . . . there's no guarantee she would even reach the Rio, and you know it.'

Kirby did know it. He also knew that they were all riding into the teeth of hell. The hills loomed large and red and deadly ahead. The sun had gone to crimson behind them, slowly sinking into the Mexican plains.

He wondered if they would live to see it rise again.

NINE

As sunset blended fantastic colors in the western sky, they began to enter the tangled hills. Red earth, overgrown with sage and sumac. The bottoms were clotted with dry gray willows and cottonwoods just coming to leaf. The travel from here on would be more dangerous. They were inviting death with each mile they traveled.

Darkness forced them to make a rough camp and after some discussion they opted for a sandy island where run-off rainwater formed two rapidly flowing streams on either side of an oval sandbar clogged with willows. It was nearly impenetrable on horseback, but they dismounted and managed to lead the horses through the thick brush until they found a narrow clearing, and there in near darkness, they camped.

Dallas and Kirby sat close together, speaking in low voices.

'We've got to know what we're up against,' Dallas said.

'I agree.' They were now riding blind into Comanchero country. No good could come of that. 'When the moon comes up, I'm going on ahead to have a look.'

'What about me?'

'I'll do it myself, Dallas,' Kirby said firmly.

Angela had been listening and she asked, 'What can

you hope to find?'

'Their camp. It must be fairly large, at least semi-permanent. Maybe with a few shacks. I want to see if there's any sign of our people.'

'How would you find out? How can you even hope to find it in the darkness anyway?'

'There's bound to be a fire burning somewhere. Even if I can't see it, the smell of smoke travels a long way. If I can find the camp, there'll be some sign that they have prisoners.'

'Such as?'

'If you have prisoners you have to keep them somewhere. There'll be indications. A shack with guards posted near it, for example.'

'What good will any of this do us?' the girl asked.

That was the main question, of course. What good would it do the prisoners to have three people, one of them a woman, out looking to rescue them when the Comancheros had twenty or more men?

'I don't know,' Kirby answered honestly, 'but that's what we've come to do – we have to give it a try.' He had to tell her, 'If it appears completely impossible, if there's no chance at all . . .'

'You will leave them! Leave Tomas to those cut-throats?'

'Your brother wouldn't want you to die recklessly for no good purpose.'

'No,' she admitted sadly, 'I guess not.'

'We have to weigh our chances,' Kirby said. 'That's what I'm going to try to do tonight – to have a look, to see what their set-up is.'

'Won't they be expecting us to follow them?'

'I doubt it. They don't even know that we're alive. Besides,' he added, 'if they did know, they'd have to figure

107

we'd be plain crazy to even consider this, wouldn't we?'

'They won't be expecting company,' Dallas believed. 'That's the only advantage we do have.'

And it wasn't much of one, Kirby knew. Still, it had to be attempted. If he felt that there was no chance at all they would just have to ride away and suffer the guilt later. He didn't mean this to turn into a suicide mission, especially with Angela along. That was one reason he had insisted on doing the scouting himself. He knew how deep Dallas's hatred of the Comancheros ran and he had grave fear of Dallas just opening up, striking back at the men who had killed his wife and children.

The moon had been up for half an hour, still low and golden, three-quarters full, when Kirby saddled the gray and led it from the island thicket.

It was weirdly silent in the dark hills. The gray's hoofs seemed to make unnaturally loud sounds over the ground.

The table of a long, low mesa blotted out much of the eastern horizon. Nearer to where he rode, the hills, eroded and wildly cut by canyons disappearing into nowhere, were painted with menacing shadows. A creature of the night bolted away through the brush as Kirby rode on.

What he was looking for was a way over the first rank of folded hills without skylining himself, without taking any trail that happened to present itself, a trail that might prove to be the well-guarded Comanchero highway to their hidden stronghold.

There was no simple way to accomplish this except to move with extreme care, striving for higher ground, remaining vigilant. Here any movement, any sound could bring deadly thunder in an instant.

Dismounting as the ground became more broken and

steeper, Kirby began the long climb. The night was cool, but perspiration trickled down his body.

Once he believed he spotted a mounted guard far across a lonely canyon, and he froze in his tracks, remaining utterly still for long minutes. He could not be sure if the man he had seen had gone away, faded into deeper shadows, or simply been his imagination at work. He decided to start on again.

Quite suddenly he came upon a narrow trail, just wide enough for the horse to walk.

He took the time to search for tracks by moonlight, but he could see no sign of recent passage. Certainly no cattle herd had been driven along this narrow trail which was no more than an eyebrow along the rutted, rocky hillside.

It was, he believed, an ancient Indian footpath rather than a traveled Comanchero road. Therefore he travelled ahead, walking the gray horse slowly, following the bends of the trail with his Winchester in hand, his eyes constantly searching the dark countryside.

Rounding a bend in the road he came upon two men and he reined up harshly.

They were fighting in the middle of the road where it widened briefly at a feeder canyon.

Rolling in the dirt, one of then suddenly clubbed the other with a bent stick and stepped back, drawing his gun.

Kirby had recognized one of the men even in the darkness and now he took a hand.

He heeled the gray roughly and it leaped forward and, as the astonished gunman turned wild eyes in Kirby's direction, the big horse's shoulder slammed into the armed man, knocking him to the ground.

Kirby, dismounting on the run, was up to the surprised

Comanchero in four long strides, and he kicked him savagely in the head as he tried to rise and reach for his gun. The gunman fell back with a groan and lay still, spread-eagled against the ground.

The other man rose shakily.

'Are you OK?' Kirby asked quietly.

'Where did you come from . . . why would you help me?' the dazed man said. Luis Escobar, with his fancy shirt torn, his hair in his eyes, blood trickling from his mouth, didn't resemble his old cocky self just then.

'He was going to kill you,' Kirby said. *And,* as Kirby had realized in the split second before he had acted, fire a shot that would bring other Comancheros on the run, but he didn't say that to the stunned Luis Escobar.

'But you are my enemy.'

'I wouldn't see you cut down in cold blood,' Kirby growled. 'Leave it at that.'

'Yes,' Escobar said. His legs were barely supporting him. His knees wobbled as he stood looking around stupidly. Finally he managed to pick up his hat, now battered and shapeless and put it on.

'He had me prisoner . . . where are the horses?'

Kirby inclined his head toward the small feeder canyon where two horses, Escobar's black and an undistinguished little dun pony stood, reins trailing.

'I tried to escape . . .' Escobar shook his head wearily. 'You *knew* the Comancheros were here?' he asked.

'Yes, I knew.'

'We did not. We were just following the herd, looking—'

'For Angela'

Escobar sighed, his hands limply slapping his thighs. 'My men . . . all dead. They are crazy these Comancheros.' He lifted his eyes to Kirby. 'And I was a little crazy too, no?'

He managed a thin smile. His teeth gleamed white in the moonlight.

'More than a little,' Kirby said tightly.

'Yes. For a *woman* . . .' He shook his head. 'I am . . .'

What, 'grateful', 'sorry'? He never managed to get the last word out. Perhaps pride caused it to stick in his throat.

'You'd better get out of here,' Kirby advised him. 'The Comancheros are all over these hills.'

'Angela. . . ?'

'She's not up there.'

'She is all right?'

'For now, yes.'

Escobar's eyes narrowed, examining Kirby. 'I think she will be all right so long as she is with you. Does she love you, friend?'

'Don't be silly.'

'No?' Escobar smiled again. 'I think perhaps. Then, my friend, you had better be careful, because she usually gets what she wants.'

'You'd better ride,' Kirby told him again.

'Yes, yes, you are right,' Escobar replied. 'How am I to explain to my father. . . ? You are right.'

Kirby watched in silence as Escobar walked unsteadily to the black horse and mounted. Then, slowly, the Mexican started riding back down the Indian trail, brushing past Kirby without saying another word.

When Escobar was gone, Kirby went to the Comanchero he had knocked down, took off the man's shirt and tore it into strips. Tying him hand and foot, gagging him, he dragged the still unconscious gunman into a clump of purple sage and left him there.

Unsaddling the dun pony, slipping it free of its bridle and bit, he left it to fend for itself. For the Comanchero he had no such pity. Someone would find him, or eventually he would get free. If he didn't, well, that was just too bad. Cold-hearted, perhaps, but he knew what sort of men these killers were, and Kirby would suffer no sleepless nights on his account.

He started on. This crazy mission had taken on new urgency since the conversation he had had with Dallas concerning Tal. He had to find out the truth. Tal, a Comanchero leader? It was absurd and he had to prove it to himself. Perhaps some other man was using Tal's name and reputation as a gunfighter to bolster his own standing among these rough men.

The trail crested out eventually. Below, Kirby thought now, in a wrinkle in the land, he could detect a soft glow as from distant camp-fires. He could not yet be sure, and so he started on, glancing at the moon to estimate the amount of time he had used already. It would not do to be caught exposed when daylight returned.

He became more sure that what he was seeing were camp-fires. Two, perhaps three, of them no more than a mile ahead.

He dipped down into a valley where fog had settled, cooling the land. Above the damp scent of the fog and grassy valley, he was now certain that he smelled woodsmoke. Still distant, but definite.

He began to find occasional oak trees now where there was water to nurture them, and soon he was moving through a fairly deep wood, oaks and sycamores mostly, with now and then a scraggly piñon pine. The trees cut odd intertwined silhouettes against the leaf-littered earth before the silver moon.

Now the scent of smoke was unmistakable. And he could smell tobacco and coffee! These scents travel further than most people believe. Ask any Indian. They can smell a white-man's camp for miles even when the fire has gone out, as a white-man's dog can detect Indians because their bodies do not smell of sugar and salt.

Suddenly Kirby came upon the Comanchero camp. He reined in sharply. Just beyond a row of oaks he could see a little meadow with cattle gathered across it, three or four buildings too large to be called shacks, too small to be described as barns. There were two camp-fires visible, one glowing softly out of view behind a low bench to his right. Around the second, more visible one, men stood or sat. Kirby could see a string of unsaddled horses tied between two large trees fifty feet or so beyond his position.

He swung down very carefully and looped the gray's reins around a low-hanging branch. Gingerly he crept forward to the very edge of the forest.

He could make out voices now. They were speaking in English he could tell by the accent and an occasional loud curse. For the most part he could not make out the words, however.

His heart seemed too large for his ribcage. He was very near the enemy, and if he were spotted, he would have no chance at all.

Sizing up the camp, he tried to figure out some way he and Dallas could approach it. The task appeared impossible, reinforcing the idea that the attempt was nothing more than hopeful folly. Yet he was determined to find, if possible, where the captives were being held.

If any of them was still alive.

He got to his belly and, through a screen of high grass, watched closely. Every now and then he would edge a little closer to the fire, knowing that those men, their eyes dilated from staring into the flames, would have trouble picking him out of the dark shadows at the perimeter. They were drinking heavily. He could see jugs being passed from hand to hand. The Comancheros' work was done; they were celebrating with whiskey – a lot of whiskey.

He heard then a familiar word and his every sense came alert.

'Oso!' one of the men had yelled out warmly and, as Kirby watched, a one-armed man emerged from the shadows to walk up to join his warriors.

It was Tal McBride.

Shock, disbelief and anger flared up and mingled in Kirby's thoughts. It couldn't be! There was no doubt that it was Tal he saw. The one-armed man with the sharp profile, the half-smile on his lips, the aristocratic bearing that was Tal. How had he come to this? Captain of a bunch of cutthroat thugs?

It changed everything.

It changed nothing – the hostages still had to be freed if possible. Kirby forced himself to get back to business.

First things first. He began trying to count the Comancheros. They shifted around in the night a lot, but there were only seven of them around the fire. Of course there would be others out guarding the road into the hideout, some guarding the prisoners, some riding night herd on the stolen cattle.

And suddenly Kirby felt some hope. Sure, he and Dallas alone could not stand up to twenty armed men, but they would be separated here and there, taking care of various chores. And if they could get just a few more guns on their side . . .

Which led him back to trying to find the prisoners. If Tomas were alive, Bull Schultz, the colonel, maybe a couple of the others, they might have a chance, a narrow one indeed, but some sort of chance.

Gliding back into the forest, Kirby began circling the camp, looking for an indication of where the men were being held. He kept the time constantly in mind. It was a long ride back to the little island where Dallas and Angela were sheltering up.

Without warning a Comanchero appeared in front of him, no more than six feet away in the night. Kirby could see his broken-toothed smile, the heavy eyebrows over wide round eyes and the pistol coming up.

Kirby leaped forward. He swung his forearm savagely into the man's face, hearing bone crack as he did so.

They went down together, Kirby on top of the Comanchero who swung two ineffective blows at Kirby before a right-hand shot thrown by McBride landed flush on the badman's jaw and he went limp and lay still against the cold earth.

That changed Kirby's program. He was running short of time now and he knew it. He hadn't accomplished much. But he couldn't hang around there now, and he began hotfooting it back toward his horse, weaving through the trees and moon shadows, his heart racing.

He slowed his pace as he neared the spot where he had left the gray tethered, then halted to look around in confusion.

The horse was gone.

'Lose something?' a familiar voice asked, a voice from the past, and Kirby turned slowly to see Tal McBride flanked by two burly gunmen emerge from the shadows and walk toward him.

TEN

Kirby stood motionless in the night, watching the three men approach. One of them was white, wearing a leather vest and a straggly blond mustache. His hat was torn and had a large hawk's feather poked into the band. The other was dark and squat, a half-breed, Kirby guessed, wearing a dark-red shirt and black jeans.

And Tal. He looked immaculate. A gray suit, the left arm of the coat pined up, clean white shirt. He was tieless, but looked as if he had just taken one off. He wore a newly blocked Stetson with a silver band. There was a pearl-handled Colt slung low on his right hip and a sheathed bowie knife on the other side.

'We'll thank you to drop that Winchester and unbuckle your gunbelt,' Tal said in a quiet, cultured voice.

Kirby complied. What else was there to do? The blond Comanchero had circled so that he was nearly behind Kirby now. His eyes glinted unhealthily in the moonlight. The 'breed was still and stolid.

'A man can't go around losing his horse, not in this country,' Tal said. He had still not recognized his brother. Kirby's face and upper body were in the shadows of a white oak tree.

116

'You don't make much of an Indian, friend,' Tal said, as he pulled a thin cigar from his coat pocket, struck a match and lit it. 'Saw you out there in the grass.'

He waved out the match and blew out a stream of cigar smoke. 'Of course we knew you were on your way. You're too softhearted. You tied Garcia up and gagged him, but he got loose. Should have killed him. He hightailed it back to camp and let us know someone was coming.'

'We all can't be cold-blooded killers,' Kirby answered. He saw Tal's eyes narrow at the sound of his voice.

'Do I know you?' Tal asked, taking another step forward.

'I don't know you – not anymore. I guess there was a time when we knew each other pretty well, yes.'

'Kirby! Good God!'

'Who is it?' the blond Comanchero asked.

'Kirby . . . it is you! How did you end up in a place like this?'

'I was thinking of asking you the same thing, Tal.'

Tal just stood there, searching Kirby's face, his eyes undergoing many changes of expression. The blond man was impatient.

'You want me to shoot him or throw him in with the others, Oso?'

'Shut up, Benny,' Tal said roughly. 'Pick up his guns. Bring him along to my house.'

'I don't get it. . . .'

'You don't have to! Jimenez, see that it's done.'

Then Tal turned his back and just walked away. The 'breed, Jimenez, and the blond Comanchero, took Kirby's arms and tied his hands roughly behind him.

'So you know Oso, eh *hombre*?' Jimenez asked, as he tied Kirby's wrists.

'Not really.'

'What was that name you called him. "Tal"? What is that?'

'The name he used to go by, to be proud to carry,' Kirby said, grunting as they tightened the rawhide lashes on his wrists roughly.

'You are lucky,' Jimenez said, pushing Kirby forward. 'Oso is letting you live – for now.'

'I'll thank him when I have the time,' Kirby said through tight lips.

They walked the short distance to Tal's 'house', a large but roughly built building concealed in a hollow of the bench Kirby had noted earlier, screened by cottonwood trees. Fifty yards further along, to the east, Kirby saw another ramshackle building – this one had two armed men in front of it. He had found where the prisoners were being kept, it seemed, but it was too late to do him or any of them any good.

A beautiful white horse with a gray mane and tail stood in front of the house, loosely tied to a hitch rail there. Kirby was escorted up onto a flimsy, sagging porch and into the shack. There, by the light of a low-burning fire in a stone fireplace, Kirby again met his brother who was now coatless, hatless. The cigar, half of its length gone, still burned between Tal's lips.

'Leave him,' Tal ordered, and Benny and Jimenez exchanged glances. 'And cut him loose.'

'Oso . . .' Jimenez pleaded.

'Now,' Tal ordered them quietly, and Kirby felt the thin, cool, skinning knife cut away the rawhide thongs. He rubbed his wrists as the two outlaws turned and stamped out the front door, closing it none-too-softly behind them.

'Got to ride 'em hard,' Tal said, perhaps to himself.

'They'll attack at any sign of weakness.'

He turned away toward a fancy bird's eye maple sideboard obviously 'liberated' from some lady's parlor or from a wagon crossing the plains. He removed a cut crystal glass and studied it briefly in the light cast by the burning fireplace logs.

'I don't know how you ever found me, Kirby,' Tal said, pouring himself a glass of expensive whiskey. 'But now that you're here, what is it you want from me?'

'It's simple enough, Tal. I was riding with that herd. It belongs to a man named Colonel Tremaine. The name may or may not mean anything to you, but he is a good friend of mine. Everything he has in the world is invested in those cattle.

'All I want you to do is let me go, give the colonel back his herd and set the prisoners free.'

Tal opened his mouth as if to laugh, but the laugh never emerged from his strong tanned throat.

He said, 'That herd belongs to my men. They worked for it. They're going to get paid for their work. We give nothing back.'

'You could,' Kirby said.

'No! If I wanted to, I couldn't. There's always another "Oso" waiting.' He sipped at his whiskey. His eyes flashed at Kirby. 'And I *don't* want to do it. Why would I?'

'I guess you wouldn't. Even if I gave you all the good reasons to do it, I guess you just wouldn't care.'

'Anyway,' Tal said, waving a dismissive hand in the air, 'don't be stupid, Kirby. These men look to me to lead them in war, not to take back the spoils of war.'

'What war?' Kirby shouted. 'You're not fighting a war, you're out murdering and pillaging! You're a thief and a killer, Tal!'

119

'You don't know what you're talking about.'

'I know,' Kirby said very quietly. 'And to think you were always my idol, my hero.'

'You don't know how it is! You haven't a clue.'

'Suppose you tell me then,' Kirby responded.

'Tell you. . . ?' Now Tal did laugh as if a 3-year-old had asked him to explain life. 'Tell you – how?'

He finished his whiskey and rose to fill his glass again. Kirby watched silently as the one-armed man performed this simple task with difficulty and, unless Kirby missed his guess, with some pain. Tal had always been a warrior. It seemed he had other, deeper wounds than the empty sleeve proved.

'I went to war for my country, Kirby. My country.' He leaned against the wall, his face cast into shadows. 'That's what they told us – go off to fight for the South, we'll whistle "Dixie" when the train brings your coffins home. I was so young and proud . . . and stupid!'

'You were young and proud, Tal,' Kirby said, 'anything but stupid.'

Tal shrugged that off. 'Then I got captured and tried to escape – you know that.'

'I know.'

'A soldier's duty,' Tal mused. 'That's what they tell you, isn't it?'

'Yes, it is, Tal.'

'Except they shot my arm off, Kirby. And then since I'd made my escape and the war was over, I was suddenly a criminal for doing what I did. Do you want to explain that to me, Kirby?'

'I can't, Brother.'

'A criminal . . .' Tal stared into vacant distances. 'I went to where I was a warrior still and not a criminal running

120

from Union law.'

'Quantrill.'

'That's right; Quantrill,' Tal said challengingly. 'And what do you know about that?'

'Nothing, really. Just what a man hears. I wasn't there.'

'That's right, you weren't there!'

'Take it easy, Tal.'

'Sure.' Tal smiled and brushed his hair back with his hand. 'I tried to go *straight* Kirby. I even became a lawman.'

'I heard.'

'Did you?' Tal's smile was rueful. 'They found out who I was in the end. They say a man can't hide from his past. I was an outlaw, a Quantrill rider, and that was that. It didn't matter what kind of job I had been doing for the town.'

'Why did you go to peacekeeping in the first place?'

'Why?' Tal's smile froze on his lips. 'It was a woman, Kirby. I tried to go straight for a woman.'

'Was she—?'

'I don't want to discuss it! You don't need to know.'

'All right. Anything you say, Tal.'

'You have presented me with a problem, Kirby. Just what am I supposed to do with you?'

'I told you. Let us go.'

'You don't seem to understand anything I tell you. Benny. Jimenez.' Tal shook his head. 'I can't do that. I told you – they'll attack at the first sign of weakness. I know them. They're coyotes.'

'And you ride with them.'

'There's *no choice*, Kirby. Not any more. There's no place for me to go. Nowhere at all except in an outlaw camp.'

'There has to be a way.'

'Does there?' Tal sneered. 'Tell me what it is then, Kirby, just tell me.'

'Take off. Leave, Tal.'

'No. I've been too long in this way of life, Kirby. Too long.'

'But the way you live . . . robbing, killing.'

'It's a savage land, Kirby. A man learns savage ways. And once you learn them, you live by them.'

They heard a sudden scuffling sound beyond the front door; a man cursed. The door crashed open. Tal dropped his glass and drew his gun in one motion. The door swung to reveal Benny and Jimenez struggling with a captive. Kirby's blood went cold.

It was Angela.

She twisted in their grip, lifted wild, shocked eyes to Kirby and tried to reach him. Kirby took a step toward her and was grabbed and spun by Tal.

'Stand still!' he commanded.

'What are you going to do, shoot me?'

'Maybe someone will,' Jimenez panted. 'The spitfire here's scratched my face,' he said, touching the red furrows running down his cheek. His greasy hair hung in his eyes. Angela continued to fight.

'Hold still, girl!' Jimenez ordered her.

'Let her go!' Kirby shouted.

'Kirby . . .' Angela's eyes were pleading.

'You know her?' Tal asked.

'Of course I know her.' Without thinking, Kirby blurted out, 'She's my wife!'

'Your . . .' Tal's eyes narrowed. He made some small gesture to the two Comancheros and they loosened their grip on Angela. She tore free of their hands and rushed to

Kirby, clinging to him. Tal, still stunned, was watching.

'When did you get married.'

'A few weeks ago, down south. I was taking her home to Texas with me.'

He met Angela's eyes and an understanding passed between them. Kirby stood, arm around her waist, facing Tal.

'Angela, this is your brother-in-law. Tal, this is my wife, Angela.'

'What is this – some kind of family affair?' Benny asked, with a dry laugh. The blond gunman's eyes were mocking.

'Where'd you find her?' Tal McBride asked them.

'She just rode up here,' Benny answered. 'Crazy woman.'

'I was looking for my husband!' Angela said, with fire in her eyes.

'You were alone out there?' Tal asked in disbelief.

'No! I was with Kirby. And our friends! Until you came.'

'I see,' Tal said thoughtfully. To Benny and Jimenez he said, 'Better get back down the hill and check her back-trail.'

'I said I was alone!' Angela protested.

'Maybe,' Tal said. 'Seems kind of funny.' Tal came nearer and stood studying Angela. 'She's a little spitfire, huh?'

'She has a temper,' Kirby answered.

'Yeah . . . Benny, I told you two to get down the trail!'

'Sure, Oso,' Benny answered slowly. His eyes were not on Tal however. They remained fixed on Angela, and the look in them gave Angela the shivers. Kirby could feel her slender body tremble.

'Well, curiouser and curiouser,' Tal said. He lifted his eyes to the closing door and walked across the room to a roughly carved chair with a leather bottom and seated himself. 'I was almost glad to see you, Kirby. Almost. I thought there was a chance we could find a way to get you off camp safely. This . . .' He shook his head. 'This changes things.'

'What do you mean?' Angela asked, suddenly terrified.

'You. Lady, to those men you're worth more than the whole herd.'

'Give me a gun and a horse,' Kirby said. Tal shook his head.

'You wouldn't make it half a mile.'

'I'm willing to try.'

'Not now!' Tal said roughly. He rubbed his forehead with his thumb and forefinger, thinking. 'For tonight, you stay here. I'll do my best to figure a way out for you.' He added darkly, 'I can't guarantee anything, nothing at all.'

Tal rose and paced to the mantle. Turning back to face them, he said, 'I'm turning in. Sorry I can't offer you my room, but I'm partial to my bed. You'll be all right. The fire will burn for a long time. There's two chairs, a couple of blankets in the closet there,' he said, indicating an alcove with an Indian blanket nailed in front of it as a screen.

Tal's own door was of heavy planks, and Kirby would have bet that he kept it locked. Reaching his bedroom door, Tal hesitated, hand on the latch.

'I shouldn't have to warn you about not trying to make an escape: there's a man outside watching. He'll shoot, Kirby.'

'I understand,' Kirby answered tightly.

'Oh,' his brother said, 'one other thing, Kirby – for both our sakes, don't try my bedroom door either. I sleep with this Colt in my hand.'

'Thanks for the warning,' Kirby said quietly, '. . . Brother.'

Tal smiled very thinly and nodded at them, his eyes lingering for a moment on Angela. Then he went into his room and they could hear a heavy bar fall into place.

Angela said nothing. She stood near the softly glowing fire, shivering, but not from the cold.

'He didn't believe us,' Angela said in a whisper.

'Who can tell with Tal?' Kirby shrugged. 'But it doesn't matter if he does or doesn't believe we're married . . . we're still in the same amount of trouble either way.'

'He wouldn't hurt you!' Angela said in amazement, her eyes searching Kirby's.

'As I said . . . with Tal you never know,' Kirby said, looking to the front door. 'Besides, he might not be able to stop the others from doing what they want. He told me himself they're a pack of animals and he can't show any weakness in front of them. Weakness might include letting me live.'

'Have they killed the others?' Angela asked fearfully. 'The colonel, Tomas. . . ?'

'I don't think so. I don't know for sure, but I saw a little shack that they're guarding. My guess is they've kept them all alive to help them drive this herd to wherever it is they mean to sell it.'

'I hope you're right.'

They continued to speak in whispers as the fire burned lower and cast wavering shadows around the room and on their faces. 'What happened to Dallas? Did they get him?'

'No,' Angela said with a shake of her head. She pushed back a strand of dark hair from her forehead and, looking a little ashamed, said, 'You were gone so long. Dallas told me to stay on the island. He was going to come looking for you And I . . .'

'Like a fool you rode along after him.'

Her eyes flashed, but she turned her gaze down and admitted, 'Yes. Like a fool . . . but, Kirby, what was I to do all alone down there?'

'You might have made it across the river into Texas.'

'I might have. But I did not want to go to Texas.' She faltered and added, 'Not without you, Kirby.'

He looked into her firelit eyes and shook his head slightly. He couldn't believe it. Was she telling him . . . no, he didn't dare hope that.

'What do we do now, Kirby?' she asked, coming even nearer, her eyes darting to Tal's locked bedroom door.

'There's only one thing to do: we try to escape.'

'You heard your brother!' Angela said fearfully.

'I know! But what else can we do? We can't stay here and wait for Tal to make up his mind. And suppose he can't hold back the others?'

'All right.' Angela took a slow, deep breath and her face grew determined. 'If you say so, Kirby, I will try it with you. But how in the world can we do it? And how can we leave without Tomas and the others?'

'We'll try to free them. I just don't know how yet,' Kirby admitted. 'It'll be risky, but no more risky than doing nothing at all. I wish I at least had a gun.'

'If we could . . .' And then Angela fell silent. Her hand was on Kirby's wrist, gripping it in sheer panic, her eyes fixed on the outer door. Kirby spun around and, as he did, he saw the latch move. The man with two drawn Colts entered from the night.

Dallas!

He was dirty, there was a cut over one eye. Dallas was to

them in three long strides, glancing at Tal's closed door. He slipped one of his revolvers into Kirby's hand and whispered, 'Well, are we going to just stand here? Let's get going!'

ELEVEN

For a moment Kirby could do no more than stand gawk-ing at this apparition from the night.

'Where did you. . . ?'

'Come on,' Dallas whispered hotly. 'This is no place to start a long conversation.'

Kirby nodded agreement. Glancing toward his brother's bedroom he took Angela's hand and they moved toward the outer door. Once out into the cool, starry night, Kirby could see but little for a minute while his eyes adjusted. But he could see well enough to see the figure of a guard, crumpled and tied up at the corner of the house.

'Come on,' Dallas said impatiently. 'I've got horses.'

'No!' Angela hissed.

'She's right,' Kirby said. 'We've got to get the others out of here too.'

'Kirby, that would start the darnedest gunfight you've ever seen in your life!'

'Maybe not. Maybe we can pull it off. Dallas,' he said, facing the blond man in the night, 'we've just got to try it.'

Dallas hesitated a moment and then said in exaspera-tion, 'All right then! Let's give it a try!'

They worked their way around toward the prisoners' cabin that Kirby had seen earlier, keeping to the shadows of the surrounding trees. Dallas pointed to where he had tied their horses. 'Just in case,' he said grimly.

In case Dallas didn't make it. Well, none of them might make it. This bordered on foolhardy, but how could he leave the colonel behind? How could Angela abandon her brother?

They halted, Dallas lifting a hand. They watched the cabin for a long while. There had been two men posted there earlier, but now they could make out only one guard, rifle held loosely in his hand, leaning against the log walls of the shack, staring out at the night in boredom. The shack had no windows, only the one door. There was a lot of open space between them and the guard. He'd be bound to see them if they tried to cross it. He'd start firing, and even if he didn't hit any of them, the shots would bring a dozen Comancheros at the run.

'We've got to try it now or forget it.' Kirby looked back toward his brother's house, wondering how much time they had. Very little.

'How in blazes do you mean to do it?' Dallas whispered, in a frustrated voice. 'Just walk up to the guard and ask him to open the door for us?'

'Something like that,' Kirby said. 'Circle your way around back, Dallas. Get as close as you can and wait and watch.'

'You gone crazy, Kirby?'

'Just do it, all right?'

Dallas hesitated for a brief second then spun on his bootheel and started off silently, moving in a crouch toward the back of the cabin.

Kirby pulled Angela near and told her what he had in mind. He could see the fear pass through her eyes by starlight, but she understood that there was no other way.

'I will do it, Kirby,' she said resolutely.

'Good girl. Give Dallas a few more minutes to get into position.'

They waited, every second seeming an eternity. Then, at a nod from Kirby, Angela squeezed his hand and she started forward, walking as bold as brass across the open ground toward where the lone guard stood.

The guard came suddenly alert. He started to raise his rifle to his shoulder, but he lowered it again. He must have thought he was dreaming or perhaps losing his mind. Here in these lonesome hills where no woman had ever been seen, came a young beautiful girl walking out of the dark night, smiling, walking directly up to him.

It had to be a dream. The guard stood transfixed. Angela continued unhesitatingly toward him, still smiling prettily, and the guard took two hesitant steps forward.

She was within three paces of the Comanchero when Dallas slipped from the shadows at the corner of the building and slammed down the barrel of his revolver on the guard's skull behind his ear and the Comanchero just folded up and fell to the ground soundlessly.

Kirby, coming at a run, crossed the yard and, as Angela fumbled with the latch on the door, he and Dallas hooked their hands under the guard's arms and dragged him into the cabin.

It was dark in the cabin, but they could feel men watching, sense the held breath of the prisoners.

'Get your boots on, boys, we're moving out,' Kirby said quietly into the darkness.

'McBride! Kirby McBride!' The hoarse whisper was the colonel's, shaky and incredulous.

'That's right. Who else is with you?'

'Me,' Tomas said. 'Angela. . . ?'

'Right here, Tomas,' she answered, and they heard Tomas sigh with relief.

'Get your boots on,' Kirby said sharply. 'Let's get going.'

'We'll need more than boots,' a man said.

'Who's that?'

'Me. Tom Peck.'

'Here, take this, Tom,' Dallas said, and he handed Peck the guard's handgun. 'Tomas? I've got a rifle for you. You might check and see if this *hombre* has any more ammunition on him. Then tie him up and stuff a rag in his mouth.'

'Cut his throat would be a better idea,' and there was no mistaking Asa Donahue's bearish growl. 'How about a gun for me.'

'I've got a rifle in my saddle scabbard,' Dallas told him with some reluctance. This was no time for mistrusting the man. They needed all the fighters they could get just now.

Kirby could see a little in the darkness of the cabin now. As they tied the Comanchero guard, he made his way to where the colonel stood shakily.

'Thanks, son,' the colonel said with sincerity. 'I'm not so sure I can make it, though. They beat me up some.'

'You'll make it,' Kirby promised him. 'Is there anybody else here?'

'I'm afraid not. Just the four of us are left after the raid.'

'Well, that gives us six men.' But it wasn't half enough, and they all knew it.

'What about horses?' Tomas asked.

Kirby told him, 'I know where their string is. We'll grab the ones we need and cut the others loose.'

'And then do what?' the colonel asked like a man with no hope left. 'What can we really do, Kirby?'

'We'll have scattered their horses.'

'There will be more guards at the head of the trail. We

can't get out of the valley,' Donahue complained.

'I think we can,' Kirby said softly.

'How!' Donahue bellowed.

'Keep your voice down, you fool.'

'What do you have in mind, Kirby?' the colonel asked anxiously.

'Run the herd. We'll have to stampede the cattle, sir.'

'My God . . . we'll lose half of them if they start running. We can't round them up again, not if we're to have any hope of making the Rio Grande.'

'No, sir,' Kirby admitted,' but we can use them as a flying shield down that canyon. If we do lose half of them – well, half a herd is better than no herd at all and us pushing up daisies.'

'It's a pretty wild thought, Kirby,' Dallas said. 'We're liable to get trampled ourselves.'

'Then give me another idea,' McBride said. But no man spoke up. 'All right, then,' he said, 'that's it.'

Kirby spoke to Tomas. 'You and me – let's Indian up to the horse string and take the mounts we can. Dallas? You, Angela and the colonel use the three horses you brought with you. Did you see that little knoll across the valley?'

'I did.'

'We'll try to meet you there.'

'What about me and Peck?' Donahue asked sourly. 'Do we just sit here?'

'I suggested you get started,' Kirby replied. 'Now – if you're going to manage to get to that knoll before Tomas and I arrive with some horses.'

'Without even a gun . . .' Donahue started to complain.

'Tom's got one, but for God's sake, Tom, don't use it unless you absolutely must! Now, get going!'

Still complaining under his breath, Donahue went to

the door, opened it a crack and, after a quick look around, slipped out into the night followed by Tom Peck.

'Dallas?' Kirby said.

'We're going. I just want to watch and make sure Donahue doesn't head for the trees. If he finds those horses we'd never see them or him again.'

The colonel, weaving on his feet, stood next to Dallas, Angela just behind, watching Kirby.

'Get going now!' Kirby ordered, and the three of them started out. Angela hesitated, returned and went to tiptoes and kissed Kirby on the cheek gently.

'Take care,' she whispered, and then rushed on to catch up with the men.

Tomas said nothing, but Kirby could see his smile in the darkness. 'Let's go,' McBride said, a little roughly, and they eased out after the others gently closing the door behind them. They had no idea when another guard might wander by, but they knew they had precious little time to accomplish their mission.

Returning to the woods themselves, they began circling north, away from the others, back to where Kirby had come upon the string of Comanchero horses earlier. They tried to move swiftly but silently. A twig broke under Tomas's boot and he cursed softly in Spanish. They spoke not at all now. Any conversation would have to be via hand-signs.

The moon hung dully in the deep sky. A faint glow glossed the peaks of the eastern hills.

At any moment, they knew, a warning cry could go up. They knew also that the horses would not be unguarded. The horses were too valuable, but they had no choice in matters now, and so they moved on doggedly through the deep star-shadows beneath the huge, gnarled oaks.

Tomas halted abruptly, putting a hand on Kirby's arm. He jabbed a finger ahead of them. They had nearly run directly into a guard. The man was sitting against the base of a tree, rifle across his lap. It was impossible to tell in that light if he was awake or dozing.

Just beyond him a dozen horses were tethered in a lazy line.

Tomas pointed to his own chest and handed Kirby his rifle. The Mexican crept softly forward in the night. The Comanchero was still silent and unmoving. Kirby's heart had begun to hammer furiously. If that man raised an alarm it would be over – for all of them. For Tomas, Kirby, Dallas and the colonel. . . .

For Angela.

Tomas was a dark ghost flitting from shadow to shadow. Still the guard did not stir. The man had to be asleep. In a moment he was in a deeper sleep.

Tomas was to the man, and Kirby saw his hand rise and fall, saw the guard slump slightly to his right, Then Tomas wrenched the rifle from the man's hands and waved frantically to Kirby.

Kirby had already started forward at a trot. Three of the horses had been left saddled by the lazy Comancheros. These, Kirby caught up by their reins. Two others, fitted out only with hackamores, were in Tomas's hands. Kirby's bowie slashed out at the hemp line holding the string and the horses were free. By harrying them without using their guns or shouts, they managed to scatter them just a little. That would have to do – they were already on the ragged edge of running out of time. They couldn't afford to rouse the Comancheros now with unnecessary commotion.

With Tomas leading the way, they started back through the deep woods. The horses' hoofs made much more noise in their passage over pebbles and leaf-litter than the two men afoot had made, but still the Comanchero camp remained still – until they emerged once more from the woods near the hut where the prisoners had been held. Then all hell suddenly broke loose.

Near at hand someone shouted and a rifle opened up from the door of the prisoner's shack. A lamp was lit in Tal's house and he appeared on the porch, firing with his Colt. Kirby went low in the saddle, firing a few shots back toward the shack. He hit only logs, but the Comanchero leaped back inside.

Now there was a flurry of rifle fire but most of it was from sleepy-headed men shooting wildly into the night. Still a bullet or two whipped past Kirby and Tomas, much too close for comfort.

The firing stopped as they gained distance, but the camp was alive with activity. Glancing back, Kirby could see Comancheros racing everywhere, some trying to tug on their boots as they ran, others waving frantic arms. There was a lot of jumbled shouting.

Then they were away from the camp, riding low across the withers, flogging the ponies with their reins. The low dark hump of the knoll was a quarter of a mile ahead across the valley floor. Running on foot ahead of them now, they saw Asa Donahue and Tom Peck. They turned back, eyes wide and frightened.

'It's me! McBride!' Kirby shouted, not wanting to catch a bullet from Peck's rifle in the night. They slowed enough for the men to clamber up on two of the unsaddled horses and then spurred on once more toward the knoll.

Already they could hear pursuit behind them, but it was only a couple of men, three at most. Those who had managed to catch up some of the scattered horses quickly, or those who had kept their personal mounts closer to where they slept.

'There!' Tomas shouted, and looking to the south, Kirby saw Dallas, the colonel and Angela sitting nervous ponies, waiting for them.

'Now?' Dallas asked, as they reined up.

'Now we get that herd of steers running,' Kirby said, still out of breath. Then to Angela, 'Stay near the rear of the herd. Ride as close as you dare. Do not ride out on the flanks. There's no way of knowing which way they'll turn once they get started.'

'Kirby . . .' Her eyes were questioning, but she only nodded. This was not the time for questions. To Tomas, Kirby said, 'Give Donahue that other rifle. We'll need him.'

Donahue took it without thanks. He had switched to the other saddled horse and he was ready to ride. He took the time to say to Kirby, 'This will never work, McBride.' He looked to the hills ringing the valley. 'If we could sneak up there, maybe we could make it through.'

'Those hills are filled with Comanchero lookouts,' Kirby said harshly. 'Don't be stupid. Are you with us or not? If not, get going and good riddance.'

'I'm with you,' Donahue grumbled, 'but I don't like it.'

Neither did Kirby when it came to that, but he saw no hope of sneaking through the Comanchero lines, nor of out-riding them. The only way was down the pass behind a wedge of hundreds of longhorn steers. He drew his pistol, nodded at Dallas, and started his horse, riding toward the milling black mass of the herd up the valley.

They hit the herd with whoops and pistol shots ringing, their horses racing out of the darkness at the startled herd. As one the cattle lifted their heads, turned and began to run, pounding northward in a thundering frenzy, heading toward the funneling gap of the trail downward.

Kirby saw Tomas, who was waving a blanket overhead to spook the cattle, suddenly jerk in the saddle and it was a moment before he realized the Mexican had been hit by gunfire. It was impossible to hear a gunshot above the roar and tumult of the stampeding herd.

Tomas hung on to his saddle although he had to use both hands to do it now. The steers clashed horns, trampled each other and surged on. The head of the trail was only half wide enough for them, and as the herd hit it they were squeezed in between the rising bluffs, bellowing complaints.

A Comanchero appeared on Kirby's right from behind a cluster of boulders, scattergun to his shoulder. Firing across his body, Kirby shot him in the chest and the man toppled backward, the shotgun going off, spewing fire into the sky.

From the corner of his eye, Kirby saw Dallas like a madman firing with both of his Colts into a trio of mounted Comancheros who had managed to ride down the herd as it slowed at the trail head. Two of them went down from Dallas's .44s, picked off from their saddles, but Dallas's guns were now empty. Kirby threw his sights down on the last man and triggered off. The Comanchero went limp in the saddle, fell to the side and was dragged by his horse, his boot jammed through the stirrup iron.

Then, amazingly, they were through the pass and onto the wider road leading to the plains beyond. Kirby reined up as the unstoppable herd thundered on, intending to act as a rear guard for the others. Dallas, too, had pulled up and was reloading his pistols. His face was a mask of grim satisfaction. Angela had begun to halt her horse, but

Kirby waved her on. Tomas, obviously hurt, shouted something in Spanish to his sister that Kirby didn't catch and the two followed the big herd on through the billowing night dust.

'Did everybody get through?' Dallas asked, easing up beside Kirby on a lathered palomino.

'I don't know. I couldn't keep track of everyone,' Kirby answered. 'I didn't *see* anyone down.' Still they waited, watching the back trail, horses and men shivering in the darkness. The longhorn herd ran on, fanning out as it hit the plains, but there were no pursuing Comancheros to be seen. Dallas was hatless now and the low moon illuminated the frown on his face.

'I wonder where they are?' he asked. 'There should at least be a few of them coming after us.'

'You're right,' Kirby said.

'Maybe they figured the herd just wasn't worth it.'

'Maybe.'

But they both knew it wasn't like that. The Comancheros might not care if they lost the herd: there were other prizes to be taken on this wide, lawless land.

But they had their code. Their pride. No man would take what the Comancheros believed to be their own without retribution. And they would come with their guns of retaliation. To believe otherwise was to dwell in a fool's paradise.

Still, as Kirby sat the shying roan horse in the darkness, he wondered. The Comancheros should have come by now with their vengeance guns. Was it possible that 'Oso' had held them back, that somehow Tal had managed to restrain his warriors from blood vengeance?

Did he still love his brother, just a little?

'Let's ride, Dallas. Let's make the Rio Grande if we can.'

And Kirby's voice was low and yet flinty in its firmness so that Dallas glanced at him with surprise, not understanding the tangled thoughts that were colliding in Kirby's mind.

'Kirby . . .'

'I said, let's ride. There's Texas, across the river.'

TWELVE

Tomas was badly wounded. The colonel grew only older by the hour, more dejected. Neither could help work the herd, and so it was incredibly tough, yet among the four remaining hands, they had managed to gather a herd of approximately 500 steers out of the original 800. Weary now, only a few of the longhorns had the urge to fight the cowboys. Asa Donahue managed to outwork even Kirby and Tom Peck, leading Dallas to suggest, 'Maybe the man still has designs on the herd. Look at him. He's worn out two ponies this morning.'

It was true. Donahue was working hard, riding the strays in, circling the herd, keeping them gathered as they crept within sight of the muddy Rio Grande, but the big man's thoughts could not be read. How he could have hopes of keeping the herd for himself and acquiring the colonel's ranch with all of his men dead or missing was unclear, but Kirby didn't discount that. Donahue had always been the wild card and his thoughts were known only to him.

Kirby worked silently, swiftly. He tried to crowd the thoughts he held of Angela out of his mind by doing so. After all, he reminded himself constantly, he was still nothing but a drifting cowboy, with nothing to offer a woman used to fancy things. He found that rather than allowing her close to him, he distanced himself from her because of that. Angela was hurt by his attitude, not understanding it. But he would not take a wife – or even think of it – until he had the means to take care of her.

'She's pining for you, Kirby,' Dallas told him one morning, as they rode side by side, but the look Kirby gave him was enough to squelch that conversation. The crew rode on in dreadful silence, wondering when the Comancheros would strike again.

They pushed the steers toward the broad red ribbon of the Rio Grande, but Kirby wondered at times why they continued. The colonel was desperately ill. Tomas had not recovered from his wound suffered in the gunfight through the gap; his face was ghostly pale. Angela spoke not at all as the miles passed. Only Tom Peck seemed to have any life in him, and he fell silent himself as the others ignored his feigned cheerfulness.

'It's Texas,' Dallas said, as the river, bright in the sundown light, appeared, and they sat the rim of the hill at dusk, looking downward, but Kirby only nodded.

It was Texas across the river, but what of it? A broken crew, a weary herd, a lost brother, Comancheros who ignored national borders behind them. Texas suddenly meant nothing, nothing at all.

'Push the herd across before nightfall,' Kirby said sharply.

'Before they drink?' Dallas asked in surprise.

'I said push 'em across. Find a ford, Peck!'

'Kirby, we ain't seen hide nor hair of the Comancheros . . .' Peck began.

'Across the river,' Kirby said.

Dallas looked at Kirby McBride whose head was hanging, his hands crossed on the pommel of his saddle, a man tired beyond the rigors of physical exertion: a man with weariness in his soul.

'Find a ford, Tom,' Dallas said. 'I'll tell Asa we're crossing before nightfall.' The blond gunman's eyes turned toward McBride, and he said, 'Kirby, you can't live your brother's life for him. All that back there . . . let it go. You got a woman who loves you. I'd—'

'Shut up!' Kirby said violently, 'Just shut up, please, Dallas. You don't know, anymore than I know what you feel about your family.'

Dallas stiffened in the saddle, started to respond and then let it pass. 'Right, *boss*,' he said with some sarcasm. 'We'll cross that big river tonight.'

And when Dallas had ridden away, Kirby regretted what he had said, but there was nothing to be done for it. His thoughts returned constantly to Tal. 'The savage way', was the way his brother had described his own life. And what of Kirby himself? Was he, too, not riding the savage trail? Where was there peace to be had in this life?

The colonel grew worse.

It had become a terrible night by the time they finally drove the Triple X herd across the Rio. The river was rising and there was a sudden heat storm, lightning flashing all around, painting bizarre pictures in the night. Half-faces, half-wild longhorns, their horns glistening in the glow of the lightning strikes.

And when they had broached the river, the colonel died.

He lay beneath a wide-spreading sycamore tree, his face pale in the strange intermittent light of the storm. Pale and weary to death.

'How many made it, Kirby?' he asked, as McBride

crouched beside him.

'Most. I'd say four hundred head got across. But the river rose quicker than I had guessed. It must be raining hard up-river. We plain didn't have the people to do the job. We lost maybe fifty to eighty drowned steers, sir.'

'Sorry, Kirby. That doesn't leave you with many, does it?'

'What do you mean?'

'The herd – it's yours. The ranch.'

'Don't talk foolish, Colonel. We'll get you home. We'll do everything you had planned to do with the ranch.'

The colonel smiled. 'You know it's not true, Kirby. My time has passed. It's over for me, boy.'

'Don't be—'

'I'm not being silly. Just honest. There's a letter in my saddle-bags. The place is yours . . . the cattle are yours. You're young and you have the right to start again.'

'Sir, please . . .'

'Kirby . . . there she is . . .' And Kirby turned his head to see Angela, fresh from the rain, watching the two men.

'Sir!'

But it had suddenly become useless. As Kirby watched, the old man died, peacefully, holding Kirby's hand. Angela went into the night to weep, the rain hiding her tears. It was a long, long time before Kirby rose and went out to dig the colonel's grave in the night, alone, using only a dead branch from the sycamore.

And in the morning the Comancheros came.

There were only six of them, Jimenez and Benny riding in the front. Kirby could read their eyes as they approached. They had not come for the herd, but for blood.

Dallas sat his palomino, hands resting on the pommel, seemingly at ease, but that did not deceive Kirby at all.

Dallas used a cross-draw and he could switch those hands only too rapidly. And he had reason enough to hate these men.

Tomas could barely stand. His wounds had had no decent treatment, but he was there, rifle at the ready. Tom Peck was behind the screen of willow brush along the river. Where Asa Donahue had gotten to Kirby couldn't guess – but then, he had never counted on that man for anything.

'Where's my brother?' Kirby asked, as the Comancheros reined up.

'Oso,' Jimenez said, 'he is no more.'

'Not *dead?*'

'I did not say that. I said he is no more. He is no longer our leader.'

Benny said, 'The man lost his head, McBride. He tried to stop us from keeping what is ours. What we have the right to. Me,' he said with a smile, 'I have the right to that girl. She is mine.'

Jimenez laughed. Dallas shifted his hands slightly. Kirby said to the mounted Comancheros, 'You know some of you are bound to die.'

Jimenez simply shrugged. 'All men are born to die. We live our lives on the edge. Death holds no fear for us.'

'I'm telling you, Jimenez, don't start it.'

'*No,*' a strange, but familiar voice said quietly. 'Do not start it, *señor.*'

Kirby glanced to his left. Through the trees eight mounted men had come silently, softly.

'Hello, Luis,' Kirby said.

'Hello,' Luis Escobar said, flashing a smile.

'This is not your business,' Jimenez said.

'Oh, but it is,' Escobar replied. 'McBride saved my life. I *do* have a sense of honor, unlike you. I wanted Angela,' he continued, 'but if I cannot have her . . .' He shrugged. 'Still I love her, and I certainly will let no animals like you hurt her.'

Jimenez looked around futilely as if he expected reserves to arrive. There were none. Perhaps some of the Comancheros had remained loyal to 'Oso' – Tal – after all.

'Well?' Dallas asked very quietly.

'You outnumber us, my friend,' Jimenez said in response.

'Yes,' Dallas said in a near-whisper, 'and I guess you outnumbered my wife and my babies. I know you now, Jimenez.'

'I swear to you . . .' Jimenez said, growing nervous. He could see that there was no back down in the Texan. Jimenez began another sentence. 'Listen, *hombre* . . .'

And then he made the biggest mistake of his short, violent life. He tried to draw his guns on Dallas.

It was so quick that Kirby was never sure afterward if he had the sequence straight. What he remembered seeing was Jimenez and the killer, Benny, going for their guns at once. Then Dallas's hands flashed and he fired with either hand, dropping both Comancheros from their saddles. Kirby winged Benny in the shoulder, but probably he was already dead. The other Comancheros, surprised, opened up, but Tomas was ready and he blew one out of the saddle and Escobar shot another one through the throat. Two of the Comancheros just spun their horses and spurred away, losing themselves in the river willows. One of them might have been tagged by a wild shot from Luis' *caballeros* . . . it was all just a blur of gunsmoke and motion.

Kirby's only real memory after that was sitting in an eerie silence in the little park as the gunsmoke slowly dissipated. And then, that sudden moment, when he realized

Dallas had been peppered by gunfire.

Blood flowed through his blue shirt. He had been hit at least three times.

'Well . . .' Dallas managed to say, bringing a blood-smeared hand away from his chest. Then he grinned and fell from his horse and Angela screamed.

Kirby was leaning over Dallas, and the cowboy just smiled up at him through the pain.

'Tell her I got 'em,' Dallas said. 'Tell the babies I finally got 'em.'

Kirby did not know what to say. Who was there to tell? He just held Dallas's head in his hands until he realized he was cradling a lifeless body.

He rose and looked back across the Rio Grande and suddenly Angela was inside his arms.

She said, 'No more, Kirby! We need a real life. Our own babies. No more of the shooting, no matter what we lose.'

But behind them the sudden violent racketing of guns began again.

THIRTEEN

Kirby had taken to his heels to race for the cottonwoods where the shots had been fired. Luis Escobar was screaming at his men.

'I told them!' Escobar was shouting frantically. 'I tried to tell them, but they had no way of knowing. They saw only a Comanchero.'

And Tal was lying shot to pieces on the ground beneath the trees.

'Brother, it hurts like the devil!' Tal said, holding his stomach. 'Funny – no one ever tells you how bad it hurts!'

'It's all right, Tal. You'll be all right,' Kirby said desperately.

'No, kid. You know I won't be. You're my brother . . .' Tal's voice was interrupted by a cough that delivered a lot of blood from his lips.

Tal gripped Kirby's arm tightly. 'No matter what, you were my brother.'

'I know it, Tal.'

'I tried to stop 'em. Some of the gang listened to me . . . I did my best to keep 'em off you.'

'I know you did, Tal.'

'Funny . . .' Briefly Tal smiled. 'It's always the way you least expect it to happen.' He winked unexpectedly at

Kirby. 'Do you know what, kid?'

'What, Tal?'

'You've got a woman. A good woman. No matter what . . . go down the trail with her.' He coughed again, heavily. 'You two aren't married, are you?'

'No.'

'I didn't think so. But do that thing, Kirby! Marry her. Take care of that girl . . . Remember once I told you I had that woman back in Lawrence? Remember . . . I could have had her if it weren't for my savage ways. . . .'

And then Tal said no more. Kirby waited, but there were no more words. Escobar came over and tried to offer an apology, but he could not find the words.

So Kirby just took Angela under his arm again and they walked away for a little while, silently watching the sun-glint across the breadth of the Rio Grande.

Finally Kirby returned to the camp and said, 'Let's get these steers home.'

So with Luis Escobar's *caballeros* assisting them, they pushed the herd of weary longhorns slowly back toward the long grassy valley that the colonel had willed to Kirby McBride. Toward *home*. But was it his home? It could be as long as Angela was with him.

'I've been silent too long,' Kirby said, as they walked out through the settling dusk the following evening.

'Yes?' Angela's voice was quiet, her face beautiful in the sundown glow.

'There was so much happening . . . so quickly.'

'Yes.'

And he gathered her into his arms and told her, 'I love you, Angela. Marry me. Help me be happy and have a real, decent life.'

'Yes,' she answered simply.

*

The next day Asa Donahue hit the herd.

How it had all come about, Kirby was not sure, but apparently Tal had counted too much on the loyalty of the Comancheros. Greed, simple greed was probably the answer. All that beef on the hoof was worth a small fortune, and Donahue hated Kirby, had from their first meeting.

But the simple fact was that when Asa Donahue did make his return, he had a dozen hard Comancheros riding with him.

The cattle, the ranch and possibly Angela were at stake. Donahue had not been willing to give up just yet. Kirby wished to his soul that Dallas was still there. Luis? His *vaqueros*? Kirby doubted he could trust them to stand and fight for his herd.

When the raiders hit, they hit hard. The first man Kirby saw go down was the loyal Tom Peck. A rifle bullet slammed into his hip, crushing it, passed through his horse's body and ripped a chunk from his other leg. A *vaquero* whose name Kirby did not even know was cut down just in front of him.

Tomas, hurting, but still valiant, turned his guns on the leading Comanchero attackers, his Colt taking two men from their saddles.

There were so many brief images, tangled and confused. Kirby wanted to spirit Angela away, but if he were not there to fight, who would? The strangest thing to him afterward was the fact that the herd did not run. The longhorns had come so far and suffered so much that they did not even have the energy to stampede. They lifted their heads, and a sort of electrical charge passed through

149

the herd, so intense that Kirby could almost feel it, but they did not run.

Kirby had his revolver out and he killed one screaming, charging Comanchero almost out of instinct. Then he felt a sledgehammer-like blow to the right side of his ribcage and he went down, hard.

He remembered hearing Angela scream. The world filled with the thunder of guns, and then he heard nothing at all for a long time.

The pain was incredible.

It was dark, silent. No one, nothing was near. Kirby was lying on the buffalo grass plains, watching stars swim overhead. He tried to think, organize his thoughts, but the intense pain in his side kept blurring his mental processes. Dallas . . . no, he was dead. Tal! And tears that normally would have shamed Kirby filled his eyes.

Angela!

He tried to sit up, but pain slammed him back against the frosted grass and red earth.

Then from nearby Kirby heard a man groan and he reached for his pistol, but it must have slipped from his grip. His holster was empty. Through the blur of pain he could now see his horse standing over him in the darkness, starlit eyes frightened and wary.

'Who's out there?' Kirby asked softly.

'It's me, McBride. Tom Peck. Don't shoot.'

'Tom, what happened?'

'I don't know . . . Kirby, I can't walk.' Peck made a deep sad moan. 'First my brother and now me! Can you walk, Kirby?'

'I don't know, Tom. I really don't know.'

'Got you too, then?' Peck asked from out of the gloom of night.

'Got me pretty good. I've got my horse, Tom. Maybe we can get aboard. . . .'

And do *what*? Two crippled-up men against the Comancheros. There was movement in the shadows and Kirby realized that Tom Peck was dragging himself toward him like a crippled dog. It seemed like hours, but eventually the two men found themselves sitting side by side on the cold Texas earth.

'Angela. . . ?' Kirby asked first.

'I don't know. You were there; it was just vast confusion, Kirby,' Tom answered.

'Escobar?' he asked next, because Luis Escobar's force seemed to be the only chance they might have of going after the Comancheros.

'He went down. I saw him. He's dead.'

Kirby was silent for a long time. The pain in his ribcage was like a red-hot boring auger, yet the bullet seemed to have missed vital organs.

'What can we do, Kirby? What can we hope to do now?' Tom Peck asked.

'We have to get to the ranch. That's where Donahue would go. To the ranch he always hoped to steal from Colonel Tremaine.'

'Assuming we could get there, Kirby, what can we do now?' Tom laughed brokenly. 'I can't even stand up.'

'I know, Tom, but there's no choice is there? I can't leave you out here. You'd be dead by morning. Maybe I can tie up your leg wounds somehow.'

'And what about you? I can't do much, Kirby. I just don't see how we can take care of each other.'

'No,' Kirby said resolutely, 'but we're not going to just lie here and die.'

Then there was a soft whistle from the darkness of the

Texas plains. Tom Peck grabbed for his Colt, but Kirby put a hand over his.

'Wait . . .' Kirby whispered. He whistled back, and a man came running toward them in a crouch.

Tomas.

'*Hombre, hombre,*' Tomas said, sitting beside Kirby. 'This is bad, very bad, no?' Tomas smelled of sweat and fear and of blood. 'Angela. . . ?'

'We have to figure they have her,' Kirby said bitterly.

'What can we do?'

'Anything but give up, Tomas. Have you got a horse?'

'*Sí*, but it was gored by a steer in the fight. He is not in good shape.'

'Well, that's something at least,' Kirby muttered disconsolately. Now there were three of them. 'Check my horse, will you, Tomas. I believe my rifle's still in the scabbard.'

'Yes, all right,' the Mexican said, but then he got a better look at Kirby by the starlight. 'But surely you cannot ride!'

'Look for my rifle!' Kirby said sharply. 'Angela's out there, understand?'

'Of course I do; she is my sister,' Tomas said, and he rose wearily to walk to Kirby's horse.

Each movement cost Kirby exquisite pain, but the three wounded men were all Angela had to rely on now. He removed his shirt and ripped off the bottom half of it – now soaked with his own blood and by the feeble light of the night skies, he manufactured ragged tourniquets from the sleeves of what was left to bind up Tom Peck's legs.

'Pretty bad, ain't they?' Tom asked, watching as Kirby worked.

'You'll make it.'

The truth was that from looking at the wound on Tom's

hip, Kirby knew the man would never walk normally again. The exit wound on Peck's left leg was not as bad. The horse's body had slowed the bullet, but still the slug had fragmented badly. It was a dirty wound, and they had no alcohol, no methylate, not even some whiskey to pour on the torn flesh. The wounds could become rapidly infected to the point where amputation might have to be considered.

'Your Winchester,' Tomas said, returning, and Kirby, rising dizzily from his work, bare-chested now, took the rifle and jacked one round through to check the loads.

'It is not much, *amigo*,' Tomas said.

'So long as I have one. That's enough for Donahue,' Kirby said savagely.

There were in fact seven or eight rounds in the tube, but, as Tomas had pointed out, few enough for any sort of gun battle. Each would have to be made to count.

'Are you ready?' Kirby asked Tom Peck, and the Kentuckian tried to grin.

'Sure, McBride. Let's get those coyotes.'

Really it was an incredible display of courage. They got Peck into the saddle, but it was touch and go as to whether he was going to pass out or not. And they still had fifty miles or so to ride. Kirby swung up behind him, and the flash of pain that followed nearly caused him to lose consciousness himself. Tomas, seemingly in the best shape of the three of them now, had been wounded and had been losing blood for the last two days. But, as he said to Kirby, 'We ride, *hombres*, right? What else can we do but sit here and die if we do not?'

And so they started forward across the vast plains, the moon rising so slowly in the east. A coyote yipped and a barn owl hooted. Aside from those sounds the night was silent and empty and promised no hope.

All seemed interminable that night. Each step of the roan jarred their bones. The animal itself was weary and hobbling. Tom Peck drifted in and out of consciousness, muttering something to himself or to his brother, Avery. Dead. That seemed like a hundred years ago, too. Time had lost any meaning.

Then there was a point when they crested a small knoll and suddenly a light no larger than a firefly flickered across the distances to meet them, and Kirby said, 'That's it. Colonel Tremaine's ranch,' and they started down the long grassy slope like a small company of ghost riders.

Reining in, the three sat the weary horses, staring into the valley below, folded darkly between the surrounding hills. Something was wrong, but Kirby couldn't put his finger on it at first. Then he was able to reason it out with a sense of elated relief, but with some deep disappointment as well.

'What it is, Kirby?' Tomas asked.

'Take a good look,' Kirby instructed the Mexican. 'There can't be more than two hundred steers scattered around the valley.'

Tomas whistled softly. 'You are right, *amigo*. What do you think it means?'

'It can only mean one thing – the Comancheros are gone. They've been paid off. They took their share of the herd and drove them away.'

'It must be so,' Tomas agreed. 'You see, there are no lights in the bunkhouse, no fires anywhere.'

Except in the big house. Only there did a light burn.

'Angela . . .' Tomas said with concern.

'She'll be there. Only she and Asa Donahue.'

'We'd best get down there,' Tom Peck said, but he was

barely able to cling to the horse's neck.

Kirby answered him gently. 'We are. Me and Tomas. I'm sorry, Tom, but you just aren't up to it.'

'No,' Peck had to admit. 'I guess I ain't, Kirby. Place me under that big oak tree, boys.'

'All right. Come morning, we'll be back for you, Tom. When this has been taken care of, I'll see you get to a doctor. I want you around working for me for a long time.'

'For you?'

'That's right,' Kirby said with determination. 'Or have you forgotten – that's my ranch down there now, Tom. My cattle, those that are left.'

'And it is my sister down there,' Tomas said impatiently.

They managed to get Tom Peck down from the horse and take him to the big oak tree. They made a pillow out of a saddle blanket and propped him up, leaving him the canteen.

'We'll be back, Tom,' Kirby promised.

'I know you will,' Peck answered, with a crooked, pain-filled smile.

They had ridden a little way down the knoll when Tomas, glancing back, said, 'It would be nice to know if we could keep our promise to Peck, wouldn't it?'

'Yes,' Kirby said grimly. Because, as much as they *believed* Asa Donahue was alone on the ranch, there was just no way to be sure what the situation was. There could very well be half-a-dozen Comancheros hiding in the darkness, watching their approach. And the way Kirby was feeling, with the injuries Tomas had suffered on the trail, they weren't a match for any healthy men, and they both knew it.

The ranch building that Kirby had approached with optimism only a few weeks ago, now stood like a menacing cellblock in the night. Still only a single light burned in the big house. They heard no horses nickering, only the sounds of the steady fall of their weary horses' hoofs.

Caution suggested that they loop through the oak grove along the pond and approach the house from the rear. Were there men looking down their gunsights at them this minute? Kirby hesitated.

'*Hombre*, we must go!' Tomas hissed with impatience. He was thinking about Angela, possibly alone in the house with Asa Donahue. But no more than Kirby was. It was just that Kirby was forcing himself to move cautiously, to make each move carefully.

They emerged from the trees and rode into the yard. Suddenly the front door flew open. It was Angela who emerged, her hair in wild disarray, backlighted by the lantern inside the house.

'Angela!' Tomas yelled, and he spurred his horse, riding recklessly toward the house.

'Tomas!' Kirby shouted after him, but it was too late. A big hand appeared, hurled Angela aside and Asa Donahue appeared in the doorway, rifle to his shoulder.

The rifle spat flame. The first bullet missed everything and sang off into the oak grove. The second slammed Tomas from his horse's back.

Donahue levered a fresh cartridge into the Winchester. It was a moment before he saw Kirby who had his own rifle unlimbered now as his tired pony charged the house. As Donahue switched his sights to Kirby, Kirby fired back off-handedly and the slug from the Winchester repeater slammed into the wall of the log house, ripping huge splinters from it.

Donahue withdrew. He tried to grab Angela and use her for a shield, but she tore free and ran toward her brother who was lying motionless on the cold ground.

Kirby raised his rifle with both hands, keeping only a loose grip on the reins and, as he fired, the unsteady horse mis-stepped and then rolled headfirst. Kirby was thrown over the animal's head, landing hard, his side exploding with renewed pain.

Donahue fired twice from the doorway, kicking up dust around Kirby, but McBride had gotten to one knee, steadied himself and fired an answering round, driving Donahue back inside the house.

Kirby managed to get to his feet and he staggered on toward the house. Angela screamed at him to run, but he ignored her call. He had come too far. This had gone on too long – it had to be ended now. One way or the other.

Kirby reached the doorway and pressed his back against the outer wall. He could hear nothing inside.

Swinging out, he opened up, sending two unaimed shots into the house. Then he breached the doorway.

The lantern was sent crashing to the floor as Asa Donahue attempted to hide in the darkness. A tongue of flame stabbed out at Kirby from Asa's rifle muzzle, sending a bullet banging into the copper pots hanging on the wall above his head. Kirby fired back again, angry at himself for having done so without a clear target. How many bullets did he have left? He couldn't remember. His head was spinning crazily.

One, he had told his friends, was all he needed. *One*, he had left probably, no more. He reached behind him, grabbed one of the heavy pots and winged it across the room. Donahue fired wildly at the clattering copper pot and Kirby McBride took his last shot.

FOURTEEN

It was a strange awakening. Kirby's mind swam with half-remembered dreams. He remembered firing his last shot at Donahue who waited, hidden in the darkness. There had been another shot, he thought, and another and then he dreamed he was taking a long swim through a darkness crowded with thousand upon thousands of wild-eyed steers. The moon had gone down and the sun had come up, but everything was still dark. A lot of phantoms had moved around him, speaking in whispers as unintelligible as a foreign language.

But he must have gotten Donahue!

Must have, because as he pried open his eyes he found himself looking toward a window alight with the brilliance of sunrise, and he could see the crows in the oak grove, and *they* were not dream-images. He turned his head just a little, and there, sitting in a wooden chair in the corner, rifle across his lap, was Tom Peck! He was a sight to see. One of his legs was splinted, the other wrapped tightly in bandage. There was a knot on his forehead and one of his eyes was black and nearly closed. Peck grinned at him.

' 'Mornin', boss.'

'Tom. . . ? Then I got him. I got Donahue? I wasn't sure.'

'Not exactly,' Tom answered with a grin. 'She did.'

'She. . . ?'

'Angela. She grabbed Tomas's gun and ran back into the house, it seems. You had just plain passed out, Kirby. Loss of blood. Too much battering of your body. I guess Donahue was standing over you, waiting to finish you off when she came in the door and finished *him.*'

Kirby half sat up. There were fresh, tight bandages around his ribs. He didn't quite understand. His head was still filled with half-dreams.

'Where did you come from, Tom? And why the rifle?'

'Tomas managed to tell Angela where you'd left me, and after getting both of you as comfortable as she could, she went out to the barn, hitched up the buckboard and came for me. Then,' Peck said, 'she drove the fifty miles to San Angelo for a doctor for the three of us.'

'Tomas. . . ?'

'He's OK, yeah. Like us, it'll take him a while to get well, but he will, Doc says.'

'Is Doc still here? I'd like to thank him.'

'Still here? Kirby, that was two nights ago! As to why I'm here, well, Angela spent most of that time sitting up beside your bed. When I got a little better, I took a turn to spell her. The rifle? Well, none of us could be sure the Comancheros wouldn't come back, could we?'

'But,' Tom went on, 'a company of Texas Rangers came through yesterday, and they're hot after that bunch. Probably the Comancheros will try to get back to Mexico. The Ranger captain said he knew you. He said to tell you that his guess was the Comancheros would abandon what they had of your herd and just make a run for it once they spotted his men.'

'It seems like I missed a lot,' Kirby said, managing to sit

up all the way. 'Do I hear someone talking in the other room?'

'Oh, *them*,' Tom Peck said, with his grin broadening. 'That ain't nothing, Kirby. Just the preacher and his wife.'

'The preacher. . . ?' And then Angela opened the door, dressed in white, radiant in the new light of morning, and Kirby had no more questions. The long night had finally ended, and the new day, brilliant with promise was just beginning.